'I'm only here for Nicky,' she reminded him shakily.

'Liar… My son was not your primary motivation,' Luciano derided in a raw undertone, thoroughly fed up with her foolish pretences. 'You came here to be with me. Of course you did.'

Jemima looked up at him, scanning the dark golden eyes that inexplicably turned her insides to mush and made her knees boneless. As he lowered his head her breath caught in her throat and her pupils dilated. Without warning his mouth crashed down on hers with hungry force. That kiss was what she really wanted…what her body mysteriously craved.

He kissed her, and it was simultaneously everything she most wanted and everything she most feared. She wanted him. He was right about that. She had never wanted anything or anybody as much as she wanted Luciano at that moment.

Ducking out of reach, and barefoot, Jemima darted round him and pelted out through the door as though baying hounds were chasing her.

Luciano didn't understand why she was running away. What possible benefit could she hope to attain by infuriating him? And then the penny dropped and he wondered why he had not immediately grasped her strategy. After all, it was an exceedingly basic strategy: she wanted *more*. And she knew he was rich enough to deliver a *lot* more.

Lynne Graham was born in Northern Ireland and has been a keen romance reader since her teens. She is very happily married to an understanding husband who has learned to cook since she started to write! Her five children keep her on her toes. She has a very large dog who knocks everything over, a very small terrier who barks a lot, and two cats. When time allows, Lynne is a keen gardener.

Visit the Author Profile page at millsandboon.co.uk for more titles.

THE SICILIAN'S STOLEN SON

BY
LYNNE GRAHAM

First published in Great Britain 2016
By Mills & Boon, an imprint of HarperCollins*Publishers*
1 London Bridge Street, London, SE1 9GF

© 2016 Lynne Graham

ISBN: 978-0-263-26392-3

Our policy is to use papers that are natural, renewable and recyclable
products and made from wood grown in sustainable forests. The logging
and manufacturing processes conform to the legal environmental
regulations of the country of origin.

Printed and bound in Great Britain
by CPI Antony Rowe, Chippenham, Wiltshire

THE SICILIAN'S
STOLEN SON

CHAPTER ONE

LUCIANO VITALE'S LONDON lawyer, Charles Bennett, greeted him the moment he stepped off his private jet. The Sicilian billionaire and the professional exchanged polite small talk. Luciano stalked like a lion that had already picked up the scent of prey in the air, impatience and innate aggression girding every step.

He had tracked her down...*at last*. The thieving child stealer, Jemima Barber. There were no adequate words to convey his loathing for the woman who had stolen his son and then tried to sell the baby back to him like a product. It galled him even more that he would not be able to bring the full force of the law down on Jemima. Not only did he not want his private life laid open to the world's media again, but he was also all too aware of the likely long-term repercussions of such a vengeful act. Hadn't he suffered enough at the hands of the press while his wife was alive? These days Luciano very much preferred the shadows to the full glare of daylight and the endless libellous headlines that had followed his every move throughout his marriage.

Even so, Luciano still walked tall and every female head in his vicinity turned to appreciate his passing. He stood six feet four inches tall, with the build of a natural athlete, not to mention the stunning good looks he had been born with. Not a single flaw marred his golden skin, straight nose or the high cheekbones and hollows that combined to lend him the haunting beauty of a fallen angel. He cared not at all for his beautiful face, though, indeed had learned to see it as a flaw that attracted unwelcome attention.

As it was, it was intolerable to him that in spite of taking every precaution he had almost lost a *second* child. Instantly he reprimanded himself for making that assumption. He could not know for certain that the boy was his until the DNA testing had been done. It was perfectly possible that the surrogate mother he had chosen for the role had slept with other men at the time of the artificial insemination. She had broken every other clause of the agreement they had signed, so why not that one as well?

But, if the baby was his as he hoped, would it take after its lying, cheating mother? Was there such a thing as bad genes? He refused to accept that. His own life stood testament to that belief because he was the last in a long ruthless line of men, famed for their contempt for the law and their cruelty. There could be no taint in an innocent child, merely inclinations that could be encouraged or discouraged. He reminded himself that on paper his son's mother had appeared eminently respectable. The only child of elderly, financially in-debted parents, she had presented herself as a trained infant teacher with a love of growing vegetables and cookery. Unfortunately her true interests, which he had only discovered after she had run from the hospital with the child, had proved to be a good deal less respectable. She was a sociopathic promiscuous thrill-seeker who overspent, gambled and stole without conscience when she ran out of money.

Time and time again he had blamed himself for his decision not to physically meet with the mother of his child, not to personalise in any way what was essentially a business arrangement. Would he have recognised her true nature if he had? He had not expected her to want to see him either, when he came to collect the child from the hospital after the birth, but in the event he had arrived there to learn that she had already vanished, leaving behind only a note that spelt out her financial demands. By then she had found out how rich he was and only greed had motivated her.

'I must ask,' Charles murmured in the tense silence within the limousine. 'Do you intend to tip off the police about the lady's whereabouts?'

Luciano tensed, his wide sensual mouth compressing. 'No, I do not.'

'May I ask...' Choosing tact over frank frustration, Charles left the question hanging, wishing that his wealthiest client would be a little more forthcoming. But Luciano Vitale, the only child of Sicily's once most petrifying Mafia don, had always been a male of forbidding reserve. A billionaire at the age of thirty, he was a hugely successful businessman and, to the best of Charles's knowledge, resolutely legitimate in all his dealings. And yet his very name still struck fear into those who surrounded him and they paled and trembled in the face of his displeasure. His loathing for the paparazzi, and the ever lingering danger of his criminal ancestry making him the target of a hit, ensured that he was encircled by bodyguards, who kept the rest of the world at bay. In so many ways, Luciano Vitale remained a complete mystery. Charles would have given much to know why a man with so many more appealing options had chosen to pick a surrogate mother to bring a child into the world.

'I will not be responsible for sending the apparent mother of my son to prison,' Luciano said without any expression at all. 'There is no doubt in my mind that Jemima deserves to go to prison but I do not wish to be the instrument that puts her there.'

'Quite understandable,' Charles chimed in, although it was a polite lie because he did not understand at all. 'However, the police are already looking for her and notifying them of her location could be done most discreetly.'

'And then what?' Luciano prompted. 'The elderly grandparents receive custody of my son? And the authorities are forced to enter the picture to consider his welfare? You have already warned me that surrogacy arrangements receive a divergent and uncertain reception within the UK court system. I will not take any risk that could entail losing all rights to my son.'

'But the Barber woman has already made it clear that she will only surrender the boy for a substantial sum of money…and you *must* not, you *cannot* offer her cash because that would put *you* on the wrong side of British law.'

'I will find some acceptable and legal way to bring this matter to a satisfactory conclusion,' Luciano breathed softly, lean brown fingers flexing impatiently on his thighs. 'Without damaging publicity or a court case or sending her to prison.'

Warily encountering his client's cold dark eyes, Charles suppressed a shiver and tried not to think about how Luciano's forebears had preferred to clear their paths of human obstacles: with cold-blooded murder and mayhem. He told himself off for that imaginative flight of fancy but he could not forget that chilling look in Luciano's gaze or his notorious ruthlessness in business. He might not kill his competitors but he had never been a man to cross and was known to exact harsh retribution from those who offended him. He doubted very much that Jemima Barber had the slightest comprehension of the very dangerous consequences she had invited when she had reneged on her legal agreement with Luciano Vitale.

Sì, Luciano brooded, he would achieve his goal because he *always* got what he wanted and anything less was unthinkable, particularly when it came to his son's well-being. If the little boy proved to be his, he would take him whatever the cost because he could not possibly leave an innocent child in the care of such a mother.

Jemima tidied the flowers on her sister's grave. Her crystalline blue eyes were stinging like mad, her heart squeezing tight with misery inside her.

She had loved Julie and hated the reality that she had never got the chance to get closer to her natural sibling and help her. Born to an unknown father and a drug-addicted mother, the twin girls had ended up in separate adoptive homes. Julie had briefly been deprived of oxygen at birth and had required major surgery soon afterwards. Her sister had not been available for adoption until her treatment was complete a full two years later. Jemima, however, had been much more fortunate in every way, she thought guiltily. Her middle-aged adoptive parents had adored her on sight, adopted her at birth and given her a wonderfully happy and secure childhood. Julie had been adopted by a much wealthier couple but her developmental delays and problems had disappointed and embarrassed her parents. Ultimately the adoption had broken down when her sister was a wayward teenager and Julie had ended up back in care, rejected by the parents she'd loved. It was no surprise to Jemima that from that point everything in her twin's life had gone even more badly wrong.

The twins had not met again until they were adults and Julie had tracked Jemima down. Right from the outset Jemima and her parents had been captivated by her lively charming twin. Of course that had gone wrong as well for *all* of them, Jemima acknowledged reluctantly. But perhaps it had gone worst of all for little Nicky, who would now never know his birth mother. Her misty eyes rested on the eight-month-old baby in the buggy on the path and predictably brightened because Nicky was the sun, the moon and the stars in Jemima's world. He studied her with his big liquid dark eyes and smiled from below the mop of his black curly hair. He was the most utterly adorable baby and he owned his auntie's heart and soul and had done so since the moment she'd first met him when he was only a week old.

'I saw you from the street. Why are you here again?' a worried female voice pressed. 'I don't understand why you're torturing yourself this way, Jem. She's gone and I say good riddance!'

'Please don't say that,' Jemima urged her best friend, Ellie, whom she had first met in nursery school. She turned to face the taller, thinner redhead with determination.

'But it's the truth and you have to face it. Julie almost destroyed your family,' Ellie said bluntly. 'I know it hurts you to hear me say it but your twin was rotten to the core.'

Jemima compressed her lips, determined not to get into another argument with her outspoken friend. After all, when times had been tough during the Julie debacle Ellie had regularly offered Jemima and her parents a sympathetic shoulder as well as advice and support. Ellie had proved her loyalty and the depth of her friendship many times over. In any case, it would be pointless to argue now that Jemima's twin was dead. Even so, the pain of that loss still made such judgements wounding. Only a few months had passed since Julie had carelessly stepped out in front of a car and died instantly. Julie's adoptive family had refused even to attend the funeral and the cost had been borne by Jemima's parents, although they could ill afford the expense.

'If we'd had more time together, things would have turned out very differently,' Jemima declared with a bitterness that she struggled to hide.

'She ripped off your parents, stole your identity and your boyfriend and landed you with a baby,' Ellie reminded her drily. 'What could she have done as an encore? Murdered you all in your beds?'

'Julie never showed any tendency towards violence,' Jemima argued back through gritted teeth. 'Let's not talk about this any more.'

'Let's not,' Ellie agreed wryly. 'It would make more sense to discuss what you're planning to do with Nicky now. You've got quite enough on your plate with a full-time job and helping out your parents.'

'But I'm more than happy to look after Nicky as well. I love him. He *is* my only living relative,' Jemima pointed out with quiet fortitude as the two women walked out of the graveyard and down the road. 'Obviously I'm not planning to give him up. We'll manage somehow.'

'But what about his father? Surely you have to consider his rights?' Ellie countered impatiently and, seeing her companion stiffen and pale, she groaned. 'My shift starts in an hour—I have to go. I'll see you tomorrow.'

Parting from her friend, who lived in an apartment on the same street, Jemima walked away at the slow pace of someone exhausted—Nicky still only slept a few hours at a time. She had expended a great deal of thought on the worrying topic of Nicky's paternal ancestry. Other than the fact that Nicky's father was supposedly a very wealthy man, she knew nothing about him or, more importantly, why he had chosen to father a child through a surrogacy agreement. Was he a gay man in a relationship? Or were he or his partner unable to have a child? Julie had not cared about such details but Jemima cared about them very much indeed.

There was no way she could ignore the reality that Nicky had a living father somewhere in the world, a parent who had paid for and planned his very conception. But she didn't know his identity because Julie had flatly refused to divulge it and there was therefore nothing that anyone could expect Jemima to do about tracing the man, she reflected with guilty relief. Her sole concern was, and always had been, Nicky's well-being. She wasn't prepared to hand the little boy over to anyone without first seeing the proof that that person would love and nurture her nephew. That was her true role now, she conceded unhappily: to step into the untenable situation Julie had created and try to ensure that Julie's son was not damaged by his mother's rash choices.

Jemima still marvelled that her twin had not even recognised that she was literally agreeing to bring a child into the world for a price. Incredibly at the time she had signed up, Julie had only viewed the surrogacy agreement as a job that paid living expenses at a time when she was short of cash and needed somewhere to live. She had admitted to loathing what pregnancy did to her body and she had not changed her mind about handing Nicky over after the birth. No, Julie had simply decided that she had not been well enough rewarded for suffering the tribulations of nine months of pregnancy followed by a birth, particularly once she had learned that Nicky's father was rich.

And what were the chances that the man would prove to be a caring, compassionate father? The sort of man who would love and cherish Nicky to the very best of his ability? Jemima believed that there was little chance of that being the case when the man concerned had not even wanted to *meet* the mother of his future child. From what little she had read most surrogacy agreements encouraged some kind of contact between the various parties involved, at least initially. After all, Nicky was half Julie's flesh and blood as well. He had not been conceived from a donated egg but from her sister's body, which meant he was very much Jemima's nephew and a part of Jemima's small family, a little connected person whom Jemima felt it was her duty to love and protect.

Jemima let herself into the small retirement bungalow that was her parents' current home. It had two bedrooms and a small garden and she was very grateful that there was enough space for her and Nicky to stay there. Her father was a retired clergyman and her mother had only ever been a clergyman's wife. Sadly, the careful savings her parents had made over the years had gone into Julie's pocket when she had pretended that she'd wanted to rent a local shop and start up her own business. Or maybe that hadn't been a pretence, Jemima conceded, striving not to be judgemental.

Quite possibly, Julie had genuinely intended to set up a business when she'd first floated the idea to Jemima's parents but Julie had been tremendously impulsive and her plans had often leapt enthusiastically from one money-making scheme to the next within days. Her sister might have seemed to have good intentions and might have uttered very convincing sentiments but she *had* told lies. There was no denying that, Jemima reflected unhappily.

Regardless, the Barbers' financial safety net was now gone and her parents' lifelong dream of buying their own home was no longer possible. In fact the only reason her parents still had a roof over their heads was Jemima's decision to come back home to live and help to pay the rent and the household expenses, which were exceeding her father's small pension. Faced with bills they couldn't afford to pay, the older couple had begun to fret and their health had suffered.

With quiet efficiency, Jemima changed Nicky and settled him down for a morning nap. Screening a yawn of her own, she decided to lie down too, having learned that napping when Nicky did was the only sure way to get her own rest. She peeled off her tunic top and winced when she caught an accidental glimpse of her liberally curved bottom in the wardrobe mirror.

'Your backside's far too big for leggings! Always wear a long top to cover your behind,' Julie had urged her.

But then Julie had been thin as a willow wand and tormented by bulimia, Jemima reminded herself ruefully. Her twin had had serious issues with food and self-image. On that unhappy reflection, Jemima fell straight to sleep, still clad in her leggings and vest top.

When the shrilling doorbell wakened her, Jemima scrambled up in surprise because most visitors were family friends and aware that her mum and dad were currently staying in Devon with a former parishioner.

That was the closest her parents could get to a holiday on their restricted income. She peered into the cot, relieved to see that her nephew was still peacefully asleep, his little face flushed, his rosebud mouth relaxed.

From the hall she could see two male figures through the glass.

'Yes?' she asked enquiringly, opening the door only a fraction.

An older man with greying hair dealt her a serious appraisal. 'May we come in and speak to you, Miss Barber? My card...' A business card was extended through the narrow gap and she glanced down at it.

Charles Bennett, it read. *Bennett & Bennett, Solicitors.*

Instantly fearing yet another problem linked to her twin's premature death, Jemima lost colour and opened the door. Julie had left a lot of debts in her wake and Jemima just didn't know how to deal with them. She shrank from the prospect of telling the police that her sister had stolen her identity to the extent of contracting debts in her name, travelling on her passport and even giving birth in Sicily as Jemima Barber. She was very much afraid that revealing that information would make her current custody of Nicky illegal and she was frightened that the minute she admitted that he was *not* her child he would be taken from her and placed in a foster home with strangers.

'Luciano Vitale...' the older man introduced as his companion stepped forward and Jemima took yet another step back from her visitors, all her senses now on full apprehensive alert.

And when she focused on the taller, younger man by

his side she froze, for he was a man like no other. His movements were fast, smooth and incredibly quiet as if he were a combat soldier slinking through the jungle. He was poetry in motion and pure fantasy in the flesh. Indeed he was very probably the most breathtakingly beautiful man Jemima had ever seen in her life. The shock of his sudden magnetic appearance was hard to withstand. Her chest tightened as she struggled to catch her breath and not stare as the compellingly handsome lineaments of his lean bronzed features urged her to do. It made her feel frighteningly schoolgirlish and she hurriedly turned her head away to invite them into the living room.

Luciano couldn't take his eyes off Jemima Barber because she was so very different from what he had expected. His very first sight of her had been her pass-port photo application in which she had looked blonde, blue-eyed and a little plump, indeed so ordinary he had rolled his eyes at the idea that such a common-place woman could give him a child. His second view of her two months earlier on security-camera footage from a London hotel had been far more indicative of her true nature. Blonde hair cut short and choppy, she had sported a very low-necked top, a tiny silver skirt and sky-high hooker heels that had showed off her slim figure and the rounded curve of her breast implants. She had been acting like the slut she was, giggling and fondling the two men she was taking back to her hotel room that night.

Now that image was being replaced by another, even more challenging one for evidently Jemima Barber had reinvented herself yet again. Possibly that big change in appearance was a deliberate element of her con tricks, he conceded. The short hair was gone, exchanged for hip-length extensions, which provided her with a glorious mane the colour of ripe wheat in sunlight. Her heart-shaped face seemed bare of make-up, his keen gaze resting suspiciously on the succulent pout of her pink mouth, the faint colour blossoming in her cheeks and the pale ice-blue eyes, an unusual shade that he had initially assumed was a mere accident of the photographic lighting. She wore a drab pair of black leggings and a tight vest top, which accentuated the sumptuous swell of her breasts.

With difficulty he dragged his attention from that surprisingly luscious display, acknowledging that the camera shots of her chest must have been unflattering, because in the flesh she looked much more natural. Even so, she was distinctly curvier. Had she simply put on weight? The plain clothing was a surprise as well but, of course, she hadn't been expecting visitors and it was possible that she dressed more circumspectly in her elderly parents' radius. In fact at this moment she looked ridiculously wholesome and young. It made him wonder who Jemima Barber really was below the surface. And then he questioned why he was wondering about her at all when he already knew all that he needed to know. She was a liar, a cheat, a thief and a whore without boundaries. She sold her own body as easily as she planned to sell her son.

Hugely self-conscious below the intensity of Luciano's appraisal, Jemima could feel her face getting hotter and hotter but, because he unnerved her, she kept her attention on the older man and said, 'How can I help you?'

'We're here to discuss the child's future,' Charles Bennett informed her.

At that news her heart dropped to the soles of her canvas-clad feet and her head swivelled, eyes flying wide as she involuntarily looked back at Luciano. Looked and instantly saw what she had refused to recognise seconds earlier, finally making the terrifying connection that set a large question mark over her hopes and dreams for Nicky. Nicky was like a miniature carbon copy of Luciano Vitale. Luciano wore his hair a little longer than was conventional. It fell below his collar in glossy blue-black curls that flared luxuriantly across his skull. He had a straight nose, spectacular high cheekbones, winged brows and deep-set eyes the colour of tawny tiger's eye stones—eyes as hard and unyielding as any crystal.

Stray recollections of her late sister's remarks on the topic of Nicky's father echoed in the back of her head.

'If he met me, he would want me… Men *always* do,' Julie had trilled excitedly. 'He's exactly the sort of man I want to marry—rich and good-looking and madly successful. I'd make the perfect wife for a man like him.'

And, of course, Luciano Vitale wouldn't be too impressed right now when, instead of the slim, fashionable Julie, he got the fatter, plainer twin, a little voice whispered in Jemima's shaken head. Was that why he was staring? But he didn't *know* that she was Julie's sister and he had never even met her sister. As far as she was aware he did not even know that Julie had an identical twin nor was he likely to know that Julie had stolen Jemima's identity. Did he even know that her sister was dead?

Jemima assumed not. Had he known, surely that would have fuelled the lawyer's first words because Julie's death now changed everything. A cold little shiver shimmied down Jemima's spine at that awareness. As Nicky's mother, Julie had had rights to her son even if those rights could be disputed in court. As Nicky's aunt, Jemima had virtually no rights at all. The only thing that blurred those boundaries was the fact that Julie had given birth in her twin's name and it was Jemima's name on Nicky's birth certificate and not his real birth mother's. It was a legal tangle that would have to be sorted out some day.

But not on this particular day, Jemima decided abruptly as she collided with Luciano's chilling dark eyes, which were regarding her with as much emotion and empathy as a lab specimen might have inspired. Nicky's father was angry, distrustful and ready to make snap judgements and decisions, she reckoned fearfully. He was not visiting in a spirit of goodwill and why indeed would he? Julie had given birth to his child and had then run away with that child, leaving behind an unabashed demand for more money.

Jemima tilted her chin up as if she were neither aware of nor bothered by Luciano's scrutiny and concentrated on the lawyer instead. The tension in the atmosphere was making her tummy perform nauseous somersaults and suffocating her vocal cords. She knew that she needed to get a grip on herself and do it fast because she had no idea of what was about to happen and for Nicky's sake she had to be able to react fast and appropriately. It disturbed her, though, that one major decision had somehow already been made and that was her willingness to pretend to be Julie for as long as she could pretend while she assessed Nicky's father as a potential parent. If she admitted who she really was, her nephew could be immediately removed from her care and her heart almost stopped at the mere thought of that happening. For that reason alone she would lie…she would *pretend*…even if it went against all her principles.

Luciano was very still, his entire attention engaged by the strange behaviour of the woman in front of him. Women did not stick out their chins and ignore Luciano when they were lucky enough to gain his attention. They smiled at him, flirted, treated him to little upward glances calculated to appeal. They never *ever* blanked him. Yet Jemima Barber was blanking him.

'I want DNA testing carried out on the child so that I know whether or not he is mine.' Luciano spoke up for the first time, startling her. His dark, deep accented drawl trailed along her skin like a fur caress and awakened goosebumps.

As the ramifications of what he had said sank in Jemima went rigid at the insult to her sister's memory. 'How *dare* you?' she shot back at him angrily, her temper rising and spilling out without warning and shaking her with its intensity.

His perfectly modelled mouth took on a derisive

slant. 'I dare,' he said levelly. 'There must be no doubt that he is mine—'

'In any case, mandatory DNA testing after the birth was a clause in the contract you signed,' the lawyer chipped in. 'Unfortunately you left the hospital before the test could be completed.'

The reminder of the contract that Julie had signed in Jemima's name doused Jemima's anger and covered her with a sudden surge of shame instead. She was about to lie. She was about to pretend that she was her sister when she was not and the knowledge cut her deep because, in the normal way of things, Jemima was an honest and straightforward person who detested lies and deception. Her desire to look out for Nicky's needs, she registered unhappily, had put her on a slippery slope at odds with her conscience. She should be telling the truth, no matter how unpleasant or dangerous it was, she thought wretchedly. Two wrongs did not make a right. This man was Nicky's father. But *could* she simply stand back and watch Luciano Vitale take her baby nephew away from her?

She knew she could not. There had to be safeguards. Nicky was defenceless. It was Jemima's job to carefully consider his future and ensure that his needs were met. But she had to be unselfish about that process too, she reminded herself doggedly, even if the final result hurt, even if it meant standing back and losing the child she loved.

'DNA testing,' Luciano repeated, wondering if his worst fears were being borne out by her pallor and clear apprehension. Maybe the child *wasn't* his. If that were the case, it was better that he found that out sooner rather than later. 'The technician can visit the child here. It is a simple procedure done with a mouth swab and the results will be known within forty-eight hours.'

'Yes,' Jemima muttered, dry-mouthed, nerves rattling through her like express trains as yet another fear presented itself to her.

All bets were off if he intended to have her tested for DNA. Did twins have the same DNA? She had no idea and worried that she would be exposed as an imposter. She lowered her feathery lashes. Well, she would just have to wait and see what happened. She was not in a position to do anything else. Arguing against the need for such testing would only muddy the waters. It wouldn't achieve anything. It would only increase the animosity and uncertainty about her nephew's future.

'So, you will agree to this?' Luciano said softly.

Involuntarily, Jemima glanced at him and connected with liquid dark eyes surrounded by black velvet lashes as lush as his son's. Her heart went *bang-bang-bang* inside her and she felt incredibly dizzy, as if she stood on the edge of an abyss gazing down at a perilous drop. Something tugged and tightened low in her pelvis and she was unexpectedly alarmingly aware of her body as if her prickling skin had suddenly become too tender to bear the weight of her clothes. 'Yes...'

'In fact you will agree to all my demands,' Luciano told her without skipping a beat while he silently marvelled at the translucent perfection of her pale blue eyes. 'Because you are not stupid and it would be very stupid to refuse me anything that I want.'

Brows pleating, Charles Bennett turned to study his client in astonishment and then his attention skimmed back to the young blonde woman staring back at Luciano as if he had cast a magic spell over her.

CHAPTER TWO

'AND WHY WOULD you think that?' Jemima fired back in sudden bewilderment, shaking her head as though to clear it.

'Because I hold pole position,' Luciano informed her with chilling assurance. 'I have security-camera footage of you stealing credit cards and using one of them in an act of fraud. If I should choose to pass that evidence to the police, I—'

'You're threatening me!' Jemima interrupted in shock.

Stolen credit cards? Was he serious? Was it possible that Julie had sunk that low while she was working in London? Jemima did recall wondering how her sister was contriving to stay at a fancy hotel. She had asked and Julie had winced as though such a financial enquiry were incredibly rude and had sulkily refused to explain.

'My client is *not* threatening you,' Charles Bennett interposed flatly. 'He is simply telling you that he has footage of the theft.'

But Jemima had turned pale as death and did not

dare look in Luciano's direction again. Proof of theft? My goodness, he could have her arrested right here and now! *Forcibly* parted from Nicky! Her lashes fluttered rapidly as she struggled to think.

'So you *will* agree to the DNA testing?' Luciano queried once more.

'Yes,' she agreed shakily.

'We will endeavour to be civilised about this matter.'

In receipt of that unpersuasive statement, Jemima's palm tingled. Never in her life had she wanted so badly to slap someone for lying. But that richly confident, patronising assurance from Luciano Vitale sent violent vibes of antagonism coursing through her and, daringly, she turned her head to look at him again. It was a grave mistake. As she fell into the hypnotic darkness of his gaze shock gripped her, tensing every muscle with sudden bone-deep fear for in Luciano she sensed a propensity for violence that made a mockery of her own softer nature. He was a man of extremes, of dangerous emotions and dangerous drives, and for a split second it was all there in his extraordinarily compelling eyes like a high-voltage electrical pulse zapping her with a stinging warning to back off or take the consequences. Seemingly he hid the disturbing reality of his true nature behind a chillingly polite mask.

'Yes, we must try to be civilised,' she heard herself say obediently while she shrank from the terrifying surge of ESP that had enveloped her in an adrenaline-charged panic mere seconds earlier.

'I can be reasonable,' Luciano declared, smooth as

polished glass. 'But I will do nothing that could put me on the wrong side of British law. Be clear on that score.'

'Of course,' she conceded, wondering why she didn't feel reassured by that moral statement.

He wanted to stay on the right side of the law. She quite understood that. Only, where did that leave her? Julie had committed her crimes in Jemima's name and the only way for Jemima to clear her name was to own up to her sister's identity theft. Unfortunately doing that would also mean that she lost the right to care for Nicky. How could she bear that loss? How could she risk it? All she could do in the short-term, she thought in a panic, was fake being Julie until she was confronted by the police. At that point she would have to come clean because she would have no other choice.

Luciano studied his quarry, his gaze instinctively lingering on her ripe mouth and the porcelain smoothness of the upper slopes of her full breasts. He was a man and he supposed it was natural for him to notice her body, but the pulse of response at his groin and the sudden tightening there infuriated him. He turned away dismissively, broad shoulders rigid below his exquisitely tailored charcoal-grey suit jacket.

'The technician will call to take the sample this afternoon,' he delivered.

'You're not wasting any time,' Jemima remarked gingerly.

Luciano swung back, eyes narrowed and cutting as black razors. 'You have already wasted a great deal of my time,' he told her with brutal bluntness.

Jemima clenched her teeth together and glanced at

his companion, whose discomfiture was unhidden. There was civilised and civilised, she guessed, and Luciano Vitale had no intention of treating someone like her with kid gloves. It was clear that he saw her as inferior in every way. She would have to toughen up, she told herself urgently, toughen up to handle someone who disliked and distrusted her without showing weakness. Weakness, she sensed, he would use against her.

Shell-shocked as Jemima was by Luciano's visit, once he had left she followed her usual routine with Nicky. She had looked forward to spending the long summer holidays with the little boy before she had to make childcare arrangements to enable her to return to work at the start of the new term. Now she was wondering if she would lose custody of him before then. She was down on the floor playing with Nicky when the doorbell went again.

It was the technician from the DNA-testing facility. The woman extended a consent form on a board for her to sign and then asked her to hold Nicky. The swab was done in seconds and Jemima waited for the technician to use the same procedure on her but instead she packaged the swab and departed, her job evidently complete. Heaving a sigh of relief that she herself had not been asked to give a sample, Jemima was in no mood for further company and she suppressed a weary groan when yet another caller turned up at the door.

Her face stiffened when she recognised her ex-boyfriend. Yes, she was still friends with Steven because her parents liked him and she had had to deal with the awkwardness of continuing meetings whether she liked it or not. Steven was a big mover and shaker in the church she attended and ran a young evangelical group to great acclaim.

'May I come in?' Steven pressed when the polite small talk about her parents' little holiday had dried up and she was rather hoping he would take the hint and leave.

'Nicky's still up,' Jemima warned him.

'How's the little chap doing?' Steven enquired with his widest, fakest smile.

'Well, his father may have turned up,' Jemima heard herself say without meaning to. That she had admitted that much to Steven was evidence of how much emotional turmoil she was in because once she had realised how much he disapproved of her taking responsibility for Julie's son she had stopped confiding in the tall blond man.

Steven took a seat with the casual informality of a regular visitor. A handsome dentist with a lucrative line in private patients, her ex was well liked by all. Jemima, however, was rather less keen. She had believed she loved Steven for years and had fully expected to marry him before Julie came into their lives.

'Yes, he's good-looking and he could give me some fun but he's *your* boyfriend. I'm not poaching him,' Julie had told her squarely.

But Jemima hadn't wanted to keep Steven by default and once she'd realised how infatuated he was with her twin she had set him free. Of course, as a couple, Steven and Julie hadn't suited, as Jemima had suspected at the outset. Her sister and her ex had enjoyed a short-lived fling, nothing more, and Jemima genuinely did not hold Steven's defection against him. How could she possibly blame him for having found her colourful, lively sister more attractive? No, what annoyed Jemima about Steven was that he was smugly convinced that he could talk his way back into Jemima's affections now that Julie was gone. Steven had no sensitivity whatsoever.

'His father?' Steven echoed on a rising note of interest. 'Tell me more.'

Jemima told him about her visitors but withheld the information about the stolen credit cards and the underlying threat, reluctant to give Steven another opportunity to trash her sister's memory.

'That's the best news I've heard in weeks!' Steven exclaimed, his bright blue eyes lingering intently on her flushed face. 'I admire your affection for Nicky but keeping him isn't practical in your circumstances.'

'Sometimes feelings aren't practical,' Jemima countered quietly.

Steven gave her an earnest appraisal. 'You know how I feel about you, Jem. How long is it going to take for you to forgive me? I was foolish. I made a mistake. But I learned from it.'

'If you had really loved me, you wouldn't have wanted Julie—'

'It's different for men. We are more base creatures,' Steven told her sanctimoniously.

Jemima gritted her teeth and resisted the urge to roll her eyes. It amazed her that she had failed to appreciate how sexist and judgemental Steven could be. 'I've moved on now. I'm fond of you but I'm afraid that's all.'

'Tell me about Nicky's father,' Steven urged irritably.

'I only know his name, nothing else...'

Steven started looking up Luciano Vitale on his tablet and fired a welter of facts at her.

Luciano was an only child, the son of an infamous Mafia don. Jemima did roll her eyes at that information. He was filthy rich, which wasn't a surprise, but much that followed did take her aback. In his early twenties Luciano had married a famous Italian movie star and had a daughter with her before tragically losing both wife and child in a helicopter crash three years earlier. Jemima was shocked, *very* shocked by that particular piece of news.

'So there you have it...that's *why* he wants a kid... his daughter died!' Steven pointed out with satisfaction. 'How can you doubt that the man will make a good parent?'

'He's still single. How much actual parenting is he planning to do?' Jemima traded stubbornly. 'And maybe Nicky's supposed to be a replacement but he's not a girl, he's a boy and a child in his own right—'

Steven pontificated at length about the immorality of the surrogacy agreement and how it went against all natural laws. Jemima said nothing because she was too busy looking at photographic images of the exquisite blonde, Gigi Nocella, Luciano's late wife and the mother of his firstborn. Luciano had matched Gigi, she reflected abstractedly, two beautiful people combined to make a perfect couple. He had already lost a child, she thought helplessly, and she was filled with guilt at her own reluctance to hand over Nicky. Who was she to interfere? Who was she to think she knew everything when she was already painfully aware that her sister had made so many bad choices in life?

'Vitale *needs* to know what Julie did to you and your family,' Steven said harshly. 'After all, if he'd kept better tabs on her, Julie would never have come here and caused so much grief.'

'That's very much a matter of opinion, Steven,' Jemima said stiffly and, deciding that she had been sufficiently hospitable, she stood up in the hope of hastening his departure.

'You're not thinking this through, Jem,' he told her in exasperation. 'Nicky's not your child and you shouldn't be behaving as if he is. If you pass him on to his father...'

'Like a parcel?'

'He *belongs* with his father,' Steven argued vehemently. 'Don't think that I don't appreciate that that child is preventing us from getting back together again!'

'Only in your imagination—'

'You know how I feel about you keeping Nicky. Why are you trying to do more for the kid than his own mother was prepared to do? Let's be honest, Julie was a lousy mother and not the nicest—'

'Stop right there!' Hot-cheeked, Jemima wrenched open the front door with vigour. 'I'll tell Mum and Dad that you called in when I phone them later.'

She closed the door again with the suggestion of a

slam and groaned out loud in frustration. But grateful as she was to see Steven leave, he had left her with food for thought. She played with Nicky in the bath and stared down at his damp curly head with tears swimming in her eyes. He wasn't her child and all the wishing in the world couldn't change that…or bring Julie back. Luciano Vitale had lost a much-loved daughter. She must have been loved, for that could be the only reason her father had gone to such lengths to have another child. Jemima wrapped Nicky's wet, squirming figure into a towel and hugged him close.

Luciano had searched for eight months to find his child. He wanted Nicky. She had to stop being so self-ish. She had to take a step back. Was she prejudiced against Luciano because he had chosen a surrogacy arrangement to father a second child? She was conservative and conventional and she supposed she was a little bit disposed to prejudice in that line. The admission shamed her. How could she have accepted Julie and Nicky but retained her bias against Nicky's father? Of course, what if Luciano Vitale wasn't Nicky's father?

Two days later, however, she received the results of the DNA testing, which declared that her nephew was Luciano's flesh and blood, and she had barely settled the document down when the landline rang.

'Luciano Vitale…' Her caller imparted his identity with a warning edge of harshness. 'I would like to meet my son this evening.'

Jemima reminded herself that there was no room for her personal feelings in her dealings with Luciano and she breathed in deep. 'Yes, Mr Vitale. What time suits you?'

They negotiated politely for an earlier time than he first suggested because Jemima knew that the later he arrived, the more tired and cross Nicky would be. And she wanted the first meeting between father and son to go well because it would be downright mean and malicious to hope otherwise. The small living room was spick and span by the time she had finished cleaning, but Nicky was teething again and cried pathetically when she tried to put him down for his afternoon nap. Ellie had been texting her constantly with queries since she had told her friend about Luciano and was reacting to his proposed visit with as much excitement as a famous rock star might have invoked.

'Are you sure I can't come round and sort of hover on the doorstep?' Ellie pleaded on the phone. 'I'm gasping to see the guy in the flesh. He looks hotter than the fires of hell!'

'It's not the right moment, Ellie. He has a right to his privacy.'

'Not looking like a walking, talking female temptation, he hasn't!'

'He may look good in photos but he's not the warm, approachable type,' Jemima reminded her friend.

'Well, why would he be? He thinks you're Julie and Julie ripped him off! When are you planning to tell him the truth?'

'When I find the right moment. Not tonight because in the mood he's probably going to be in he's likely to just scoop up Nicky and walk straight out of here with him,' Jemima admitted with a grimace.

'Whether Luciano Vitale knows it or not, he owes you,' Ellie said loyally. 'Julie couldn't cope with Nicky and you've been caring for him since he was only a week old. Your parents will miss him terribly, though, when he goes.'

When he goes, Jemima repeated inwardly, her heart sinking as she was finally forced to face that certainty. Nicky was about to be taken away from her and there was not one blasted thing she could do about it. She was not Nicky's closest relative, Luciano was.

Jemima was very tense while she waited for her visitor. Nicky looked adorable in a little blue playsuit but he was teething and in a touchy temperamental mood in which he could travel from smiles to tears in the space of seconds.

Jemima heard the cars arrive and rushed to the window. The equivalent of a cavalcade had drawn up outside on the street, a collection of vehicles composed of a black limousine and several Mercedes cars, all with tinted windows. As she watched several men emerged from the accompanying cars and fanned out across the street while clearly taking direction from ear devices. All the men wore formal suits and sunglasses and emanated an aggressive take-charge vibe. Finally the rear door of the limo was opened and Luciano slid out, instantly casting everyone around him in the shade. He wore well-washed jeans and a long-sleeved black sweater...and still, he took her breath away.

The well-cut denim outlined long, powerful thighs

and lean hips, while the dark sweater somehow enhanced his blue-black hair and olive skin. Her mouth
ran dry while she stared and smoothed damp palms
down over her own, more ordinary jeans, wishing she
had the same sleek, fashionable edge he exuded with
infuriating ease. As she began to back away from the
window a movement behind him attracted her attention and she stared as a slim blonde woman climbed
out of the car. Instantly, Luciano turned to speak to the
woman and a moment later she got back into the car,
evidently having thought better of accompanying him.
Who was she? His girlfriend?

It's none of your business who she is, a voice re-
proved in Jemima's mind and she moved through to
the doorway and breathed in deep, struggling to bol-
ster herself for what was to come. She opened the door
briskly. 'Mr Vitale…'

'Jemima,' he said drily, stepping inside, his sculpted
lips unsmiling, an aloof coolness stamped across his
lean bronzed face like a wall.

'Nicky's in here…' Jemima pressed the living-room
door wider to show off Nicky where he sat on the floor
surrounded by his favourite toys.

'His name is Niccolò,' Luciano corrected without
hesitation. 'I don't like diminutives. I would also like
to meet my son alone…'

Jemima glanced up at him in surprise and dismay
but he wasn't looking at her. His attention was all for
Nicky, no, Niccolò, and Luciano's lustrous tiger eyes
were gleaming as he literally savoured his first view of
his son with an intensity she could feel. Jemima stared,

couldn't help doing it, noting with relief that the forbidding lines of Luciano's lean dark face were softening, the hard compression of his beautifully sculpted hard mouth easing.

'Thank you, Miss Barber,' Luciano Vitale murmured, deftly planting himself inside the room and leaving her outside as he firmly closed the door in her face.

With a sigh, Jemima sat down on the phone bench just inside the front door. Of course he didn't want an audience, she reasoned, striving to be fair and reasonable. Who was the woman waiting outside for Luciano? If she was his girlfriend, did he live with her? Was it possible that the girlfriend was unable to have children and that she and Luciano had entered the surrogacy agreement as a couple? And what did any of those facts matter to her? Well, they mattered, she conceded ruefully, because she cared a great deal about Nicky's future but ultimately she had no say whatsoever in what came next.

As a whimper sounded from the living room Jemima tensed. Nicky was going through a stranger-danger phase. She could hear the quiet murmur of Luciano's voice as he endeavoured to soothe the little boy. Sadly, a sudden outburst of inconsolable crying was his reward. Jemima made no move but her hands were clenched into fists and her knuckles showed white beneath her pale skin as she resisted the urge to intervene. The sound of Nicky becoming increasingly upset distressed her but she knew she had to learn to step back and accept that Luciano Vitale was Nicky's father and his closest relative.

When Nicky's sobs erupted into screams, the living-room door opened abruptly. 'You'd better come in... He's frightened,' Luciano bit out in a harsh undertone.

Jemima required no second invitation. She scrambled up and surged past him. Nicky's anxious eyes locked straight on to her and he held up his arms to be lifted. Jemima crouched down to scoop him up and he clung like a monkey, shaking and sobbing, burying his little head in her neck.

Luciano watched that revealing display in angry disbelief. Niccolò had two little hands fisted in his mother's shirt, his fearful desperation patently obvious as he hid his face from the stranger who had tried to make friends with him. As Jemima quieted the trembling child Luciano registered two unwelcome facts. His son was much more attached to his mother than his father had expected and Jemima was very definitely the centre of his son's sense of security. It was a complication he neither wanted nor needed. His attention dropped to the generous curve of Jemima's derriere in jeans and he tensed, averting his gaze to the back of his son's curly head as he felt himself harden. So, he liked women to look more like women than slender boys and she had splendid curves, but he abhorred that hormonal response that was so very inappropriate in Jemima Barber's radius.

'He's teething, which always makes him a bit clingy,' Jemima proffered in Nicky's defence. 'And this is the wrong end of the day for him because he's tired and fractious—'

'He's terrified. Isn't he used to meeting people?' Luciano pressed critically.

'He's more used to women.'

'But your parents must've been looking after him for you while you were in London,' he pointed out, momentarily depriving her of breath as he reminded her of the lie she was living for his benefit. After all, nobody could be in two places at once and while Jemima had been teaching and covering Nicky's childcare costs at a local nursery facility, Julie *had* been in London.

'Dad's retired but he's still out and about a lot, so Nicky would've seen less of him,' Jemima muttered in a brittle voice, crossing her fingers at a lie that made her feel guiltier than ever because Nicky adored his grandfather.

Nicky stuck his thumb in his mouth and sagged against Jemima with a final hoarse whimper. 'Sorry about this…' she added uncomfortably. 'But in time he'll get used to you.'

Luciano compressed his lips. He didn't have time to waste.

'Is that your girlfriend outside waiting in the car?' Jemima asked abruptly, keen to know and to change the subject about Nicky's lifestyle in recent months.

Luciano frowned, winged ebony brows pleating above hard dark eyes fringed by lashes as dense and noticeable as black lace. 'No, the nanny I'm hiring.'

Jemima stopped breathing. 'A nanny?' she gasped in dismay.

'I will need some support in caring for my son,' Luciano countered drily, wondering what he was going to do about the problem his son's mother had become.

Well, he certainly wouldn't be marrying her as Charles Bennett had ludicrously suggested after the results of the DNA test had been revealed.

'A paper marriage,' Charles had outlined. 'In one move you would legitimise your son's birth, tidy up any future inheritance issues and gain a legal right to have custody of your son. As an ex-wife you could also give her a settlement without breaking the law. It would be perfect.'

Perfect only in a nightmare, Luciano reflected grimly. No way was he linking his name to a woman who was no better than a thieving hooker, not in a paper marriage of any kind.

He was employing a nanny, Jemima thought wretchedly as panic snaked through her in a cold little shiver of foreboding. Clearly Luciano was planning to remove Nicky from her care as soon as he could.

Luciano surveyed his infant son, who was engaged in contentedly falling asleep against his mother's shoulder. He could rip him away from Jemima as he himself had once been ripped away from his own mother. All right, he had been almost three years old but he had never forgotten the day he was torn from his mother's loving arms. Of course there had been a lot of blood and violence involved and naturally he had been traumatised by the episode. He would not be doing anything of that nature. He despised Jemima Barber but he did not wish her dead for having crossed him. At the same time, however, he deeply resented her hold on his son.

'Nicky's very emotional,' Jemima remarked cautiously. 'He does get upset quite easily.'

'I'm surprised he's so fond of you. You've spent most of your time in London and left other people looking after him,' Luciano condemned.

'I've spent much more time with him than you appreciate,' Jemima protested, tilting her chin. 'Of course he's fond of me...'

'But you always planned to give him away,' he reminded her coolly. 'As long as the pay-off was sufficient. Shouldn't you have prepared him better for the separation?'

An angry flush illuminated her pale porcelain skin. 'I didn't know if there was going to *be* a separation!' she fired back awkwardly.

'I would let nothing prevent me from claiming my son. Since you disappeared there has not been a single day that I haven't thought of him,' Luciano proclaimed, dark honey-rich eyes glittering with challenge. 'He is mine—'

'Yes...' she conceded raggedly, her breath catching in her throat below the onslaught of his extraordinarily compelling gaze. 'But handing him over isn't going to be as simple...er...as I once thought it would be.'

Luciano shrugged a broad shoulder without interest. 'You convinced a psychiatrist that you knew what you were signing up to do and could cope with it.'

Desperation slivered through Jemima's taut frame. 'Things change...' she whispered.

'I want my son,' Luciano told her bluntly.

The germ of a wild idea burst into being inside Jemima and flew straight from brain to tongue without the benefit of any filter or forethought. 'Couldn't *I* be your nanny? Even for a little while?'

Luciano studied her in disbelief. 'My nanny? *You?* Are you crazy?'

'Only until he settles into his new life. You'd be getting a trained infant teacher to look after him. I'm well qualified with young children.'

'But you've never worked with them?'

'Of course I have work experience.'

'Before you decided that you much preferred earning easy money as an escort?'

Jemima froze. 'An...*es-escort*?' Her voice stumbled over the mortifying word. 'That's a dreadful—'

Luciano sighed. 'I know everything about you. You can't lie to me. You were working as an escort in London and you were very popular with older men until you began to steal their wallets. I spoke to the agency that made your bookings for you before deciding to dispense with your services.'

Her lips parted and then closed again. She had turned white as snow, shock thudding through her, her heart thumping loudly in her eardrums. She didn't want to believe him but she did because Julie's love of money had been much stronger than her self-respect. An escort? An escort offering extras? Jemima squirmed, raw humiliation bowing her head. Working as an escort had given her twin the chance to steal. And sadly, the stolen credit cards had only been the tip of the iceberg, she acknowledged wretchedly. Seemingly Julie had been as willing to sell herself as she had been to sell her son.

'It was an exclusive escort service,' Luciano conceded, recognising her mortification and less gratified by it than he had expected to be.

'So I wouldn't be quite what you want in a nanny,' Jemima breathed, stricken, receiving that message loud and clear from his attitude.

'I'm afraid not. My security team will pick Niccolò up tomorrow and bring him up to London for the day. I'll send the nanny with them.' Luciano read her consternation with ease. 'Naturally I want to spend time with my son.'

'Before you do...*what*?' Jemima pressed helplessly.

'Before I take him home to Sicily with me,' Luciano fielded. 'You know how this must end, Jemima. Why make it more difficult for all of us?'

Jemima subsided like a pricked balloon. Julie had accepted payment and signed the agreement. There was no escape clause unless she was willing to run screaming to the media with her sad story. And where would that get her? More importantly, what would it gain Nicky? Notified of the circumstances of Nicky's birth, the social services would probably step in to take charge of Nicky and decide his future and there was no guarantee that Luciano would get him either. In fact there was every chance that Nicky would be placed in an adoptive home and neither Jemima nor Luciano would ever see him again. Seeking outside help would be the wrong thing to do, she decided in despair. The very fact she had lied and faked being

Julie to hold on to her nephew would be held against her by the authorities...and by Luciano if he ever found out the truth.

CHAPTER THREE

'So COULD I have a lift with you up to London?' Jemima asked the nanny cheerfully. 'I assure you that a lift is all I want, but my being in the car will make it easier for you to get to know Nicky and I can run through his routine with you as well.'

'Er... I...' Nonplussed, the nanny, who had introduced herself as Lisa, hovered on the doorstep and looked at the tall, broadly built bodyguard standing behind her for direction.

The bodyguard dug out a cell phone and punched in a number and Jemima got the obvious message: nothing could be done because no plan could deviate in the smallest way without Luciano Vitale's permission and approval. She scolded herself for thinking that she was being clever when she had come up with the idea the night before. Yet she truly wasn't trying to interfere with Luciano's day with Nicky. She simply wanted to be more accessible if anything went wrong.

'I just thought I could take the opportunity to do some shopping,' she fibbed nervously as the bodyguard's conversation in staccato Italian continued at length.

'Mr Vitale makes all the arrangements,' Lisa told her with an apologetic smile. 'I don't want to screw up my first day on the job. It would be handy, though, to know a little more about your son.'

'Miss Maurice?' The bodyguard handed the phone to the nanny.

Jemima watched the woman stiffen, straighten her shoulders and pale as she evidently received her instructions while answering yes and no several times. She then extended the phone to Jemima.

Realising that it was now her turn to receive her orders, Jemima laughed out loud, stunning her companions.

'So glad you've found something to laugh about today,' Luciano drawled, sharp and swift as a stiletto stabbing at her down the line.

'Oh, please don't take it like that,' Jemima babbled in dismay. 'I promise you that you won't see or hear from me today. I just want to be in London...to...er... shop—'

'I can hear the lie in your voice—'

Her blood ran cold in her veins.

'You got a sixth sense or something?'

'Or something. Tell me the truth or I will not consider the idea,' he told her coldly.

'I wanted to be within reach...you know, in case you needed me. That's all.'

At his end of the line, Luciano gritted his perfect white teeth. Where the hell did she get the nerve to bug him like this? He expelled his breath in a hiss of impatience. 'Why would I need you?'

'Not you, *him*,' Jemima stressed. 'And dial back the tension, Luciano. Nicky can be very temperamental. He works best with calm, quiet and soothing—'

Luciano was incredulous. 'Let me get this straight— *you* are telling *me* how to behave?'

'But not in a rude way, in a *helpful* way,' Jemima emphasised.

'You are irritating me,' Luciano growled soft and low.

'Ditto.' Jemima groaned out loud, having forgotten her audience. 'Less of the growly stuff would be nice but not if you replace it with the rave-from-the-grave voice.'

The rave from the grave, Luciano mouthed in silent disbelief. She was actually telling him that he irritated her. How dared she? A thieving whore…but the *mother* of his *son*…

'You can travel to London with them and accompany Niccolò back again at five today. Pass the phone back to Rico…'

Jemima did as she was bid, handing Nicky's baby bag to the second bodyguard who had appeared before tucking her nephew under her arm to lock up the house.

'What a fuss about nothing,' she wanted to remark to the nanny as she climbed into the limousine and the two women together secured the baby into the very fancy car seat awaiting him, but caution silenced her. Luciano was an intractable tyrant supported in his moods and habits by his intimidated employees. Presumably standing up to Luciano meant instant dismissal. Jemima suspected she wouldn't last five minutes working for him because she had too much a mind of her own, so it was probably fortunate that he hadn't jumped on her nanny offer. At the same time, however, she was relieved he had agreed to let her catch a lift to London and travel back with Nicky at the end of the day. She had been a tiny bit afraid that Luciano wasn't planning on letting Nicky return to her again and now that looming fear could be set aside for at least one more day. Having passed her cell-phone number to Lisa, she asked to be dropped at the entrance to a Tube station.

The attraction of browsing round shops where she could not afford to buy anything held little appeal for Jemima. In recent months she had grown accustomed to being stony broke, to questioning every single purchase and asking herself if she really needed the item. And although she would have adored some new clothes and the chance to replace cosmetics that had run out, she was happy to make those sacrifices to keep Nicky and give her parents peace of mind in their retirement. A desire to make the best of whatever life threw at her had always driven Jemima and she took the same approach to her day out, heading to the first of her free attractions—the British Museum—before enjoying a picnic lunch in Kensington Gardens and a walk round the Tate Modern. She was on the banks of the Thames when her phone rang and she snatched it out.

'Nicky's ill... Where are you?' Luciano demanded thinly. 'I'll have you picked up.'

Her frantic questions elicited no adequate response beyond the assurance that the baby was not in danger. Luciano was much more intent on retrieving her as soon as possible so that she could comfort the little boy. Jemima was perspiring with stress and anxiety by the time a limousine lifted her at the agreed pick-up point and drove her across London to an exclusive block of apartments. There, flanked by two enormous bodyguards, she got into a glass lift to be swept up to the penthouse.

'I thought you were going to stay within reach!' Luciano roared at her as she came through the front door.

Jemima was accustomed to dealing with distraught and often angry parents whose child had become upset at school or had suffered injury and at one glance she recognised that Luciano fell into that category. He was a powerful man who controlled everything around him but Nicky's illness had made him feel powerless and that anger was the fallout. She could hear Nicky's distressed choking wails echoing through the apartment and was not in the mood to waste time sparring with his anxious father. 'Where is he?'

'The doctor's with him,' Luciano gritted, closing a managing hand to her spine to herd her in the right direction. He was the most alarmingly dominant man and, even worse, she thought ruefully, it seemed to come entirely naturally to him, as if an autocratic need to trample over the little people had been programmed into him at birth. 'Not that he's been much use!'

Lisa was pacing the floor with a wailing Nicky and looked as though she had been through the wars. Earlier that day she had looked immaculate. Now her long hair was falling down untidily and her shirt was spattered with food stains. An older bespectacled man, who could only be the doctor, overlooked the scene with an air of discomfiture.

'What's wrong with Nicky?' Jemima asked worriedly.

The doctor studied her anxiously. 'A touch of tonsillitis…nothing more—'

'My son would not be making such a fuss over so little,' Luciano began wrathfully.

'Oh, yes, he would.' Jemima threw Luciano a wryly apologetic glance. 'He makes a real fuss when he's sick. He's had tonsillitis a couple of times already and I was up all night with him.'

With a yell, Nicky unglued his reddened eyes and, focusing joyously on Jemima, he gave a frantic lurch in Lisa's hold. The other woman crossed the room in haste to settle him into Jemima's arms. 'It's obvious he wants his mum.'

'Perhaps you could explain to…er…Nicky's father that this is not a serious condition. The baby has a mild fever and a sore throat and possibly some ear pain.' Exhausted, Nicky moaned against Jemima's shoulder, his solid little body heavy against her as he slumped.

'Try to get him to drink some water to keep him hydrated,' the doctor advised with a wary glance in Luciano's smouldering direction. 'Within a couple of days and with the medication he'll soon be back to normal.'

'Thank you,' Jemima pronounced quietly as she

sank down on a comfortable leather seat and accepted the baby bottle of water Lisa helpfully extended. She studied Nicky and glanced across the room at Luciano. So, she finally had first-hand evidence of whose genes had dealt Nicky the theatrics and the fireworks, she thought wryly, ignoring Nicky when he twisted away his mouth from the bottle. 'Do you want your cup?' she asked.

Nicky looked up at her, dark eyes cross and shimmering with tears.

Jemima dug the baby cup out of the bag and proceeded to pour some water into it while still cradling Nicky.

'Seems that he is one little boy who knows what he wants,' Lisa remarked.

'You're spot on.' Jemima watched the baby moisten his lips and then try a tiny sip. Forced to swallow, he grimaced and sobbed again while she praised him and told him what a brave, wonderful boy he was.

Luciano watched the performance unfolding with blazing dark golden eyes, angry frustration assailing him. He knew when he was facing a fait accompli. Jemima handled Nicky beautifully, clearly knew him inside out and responded smoothly to his needs. He himself and the highly qualified nanny had failed utterly to provide the comfort his son had needed. He wondered if little boys were programmed to want mothers over father figures. He wondered tensely how his son would cope without a mother, particularly with her sudden disappearance. Bemused by that flood of concern and the sort of deep questions he normally suppressed, Luciano grated his teeth together in frustration and called someone to show out the doctor.

'It *is* only a mild illness,' Jemima remarked quietly. 'Relax.'

'How the hell am I supposed to relax when my son is suffering?' Luciano lashed back at her in fierce attack.

'Sometimes you *can't* fix things and the normal childhood illnesses fall into that category,' Jemima pointed out gently.

Well, he *cared* about Nicky; he was quite accidentally revealing that with his behaviour. Of course, he had to be aggressive even in that, but then he was an aggressive man. And intelligence warned her that Luciano Vitale would not voluntarily share anything with her that he considered to be private or personal. Obviously his feelings about his son would fall squarely into that territory and it was not for her to pry, she told herself doggedly as Nicky snuffled into an exhausted sleep on her lap.

Luciano strode to the door, raking an impatient hand through his blue-black glossy hair. A dark shadow of stubble outlined his sculpted mouth and strong jawline. He was obviously the sort of man who had to shave twice a day. He had loosened his racy red tie at the collar, unbuttoned the top button of his white shirt. He looked a little more human and a little less perfect than at their previous meeting and she censured her selfish sense of satisfaction that he was finding his son more of a challenge than he had expected. Such a feeling was mean and ungenerous, she reminded herself angrily. Nicky was Luciano's flesh and blood and she should be pleased that he was so keen to get to know his child.

Lisa reappeared and hovered.

'The nanny will put my son in his cot for a nap now,' Luciano announced. 'We have to talk.'

Talk? What about? A frown indented Jemima's brow as she passed her nephew carefully over to the young woman and the door closed in their wake.

'What do you want to discuss?' she asked stiffly.

Luciano shot her a chilling appraisal. 'Oh, please, don't come over all naïve on me now. I prefer honesty. You've made it clear that you want to make the most profit you can from having brought my child into the world,' he pointed out with unconcealed contempt. 'But I simply want what makes my son happy and it is patently obvious that in the short-term at least Niccolò will not be happy if you suddenly vanish from his life.'

Jemima studied him, surprised he was willing to admit that possibility.

'Although there is nothing I can like, respect or admire about you, Jemima...my son *is* attached to you,' he conceded in a grim-mouthed tone of finality. 'I do not want to damage him by immediately forcing you out of his life. He deserves more consideration from me. After all, he did not choose the unusual circumstances of his birth—*I* did.'

His ringing assurance that he did not like, respect or admire her cut Jemima surprisingly deep and yet she was wryly amused by her apparent vulnerability towards his low opinion of her morals. He thought she was Julie and while she faked being Julie she had to own her sister's mistakes and pay the price of them too.

Luciano watched her porcelain-fair skin wash a guilty pink that simply accentuated the ice-blue eyes, which reminded him of very pale aquamarines he had once glimpsed in his mother's jewellery box. Those eyes and that full, soft pillowy mouth were snares that any man would zero in on, he told himself, his attention widening its scope to encompass the full, buoyant swell of her breasts below the simple tee she wore. He wondered what colour her bra was and marvelled at the ludicrous thought. What was he? A randy school-boy? He had access to many sexual choices and almost any one of those women would be classier, safer and more beautiful than Jemima Barber, he reminded himself impatiently. Even so, it was his son's mother who was making him hard and taut and needy where it mattered, when he was all too often indifferent to female fawning and flirtation.

But then possibly what annoyed him most about Jemima was that he had yet to see any sign that she was making the smallest effort to sexually attract him. She did not appear to be wearing make-up and her plain denim skirt came to her knees while she sat with her pale slim legs neatly and modestly folded to one side. It was like a simulated virginal act, he reasoned in exasperation. Possibly she had already worked out that hooker heels and too much exposed female flesh were not his style.

Sex was no big deal, he thought impatiently. That was a truth he had embraced long ago. He didn't make time for sex, though, and perhaps that explained his reaction to his son's mother. Possibly any reasonably appealing woman would have given him the same response. But the nanny did nothing for his libido, he conceded, and neither did any of the very attractive female staff he employed. No, Jemima Barber had something special about her, something insidiously sexy he had yet to pin down and label, and it drew him like a very strong magnet. And he loathed it, loathed it like poison in his system, because she was everything he despised in a woman.

The silence smouldered like a simmering pot on a gas hob. Jemima could feel heat striking through her, spreading up from the warmth in her pelvis. *He* did that to her. *He* made her tummy fill with butterflies. *He* made an embarrassing hot, slick sensation pulse between her thighs. *He* made her nipples tighten and push against the barrier of her bra.

That reality mortified and shamed her and reminded her of her first crush as a teenager when her body had gone haywire with a physical longing she hadn't understood and hadn't really been ready to embrace. But this was different because those responses were now attacking her adult body. She found herself studying that gorgeous face of his even though she didn't want to stare, didn't want to notice the perfection of his sleek cheekbones, the classic jut of his nose or the strong line of the jaw cradling that superbly masculine mouth. And then she fell into the dark and dangerous enticement of his deep-set eyes that were tigerish gold in the light from the window and once she looked she couldn't breathe, couldn't think, couldn't even function, she thought in bemused dismay.

The door opened and an older woman came in carrying a tray. Coffee was poured. Luciano took his black and without sugar. Jemima took hers milky and sweet, their differences as pronounced in coffee as in everything else.

Cradling his cup in one elegant, long-fingered hand, Luciano murmured, 'I've decided that I want you to accompany us to Sicily as the nanny you offered to be...'

Shock made Jemima's lower lip part from her upper and she breathed again and a little faster, her eyes widening at that bombshell of a suggestion.

'It would ease the transition for my son but it would be on the strict understanding that you would begin stepping back from him while allowing others to step forward to take your place in his little world,' Luciano spelt out coolly. 'He must learn to do without you.'

Jemima tried and failed to swallow as he described the role. He had delivered the killing blow of truth by telling her what he ultimately expected and wanted from her. Sicily and the nanny job would be very temporary for her and would come at a high cost for a woman who loved the child she cared for. She lost colour, pain knotting inside her at the prospect of walking away from Nicky, but at the same time with every word Luciano Vitale spoke she saw that whether she liked it or not he was worthy of her respect as a father. He detested her yet he still recognised the strength of her bond with his son and he was keen to protect Nicky from getting hurt. How could she judge him badly for that? A more gradual process of parting Jemima from her nephew *should* work much better than a sudden break, she reasoned unhappily. Luciano was taking the sensible, cautious approach to the problem.

Her silence perturbed Luciano, who had expected instant eager agreement. Didn't Jemima Barber worship money and the high life? Wasn't she a fish out of water in her parents' modest home? He had assumed that was why she had made the strange offer to take on the role of acting as her son's nanny. After all, only that position would grant her entry into Luciano's wealthy, exclusive and privileged world. She was also broke, in debt and had to be afraid of the police catching up with her, so a trip abroad should have all the appeal of an escape hatch.

'Have you changed your mind about that offer?' Luciano asked in surprise.

'Well, it was an impulse of the moment offer,' Jemima admitted ruefully. 'I didn't really think it through. It was provoked by the prospect of parting from Nicky—'

'Sicily may make the process a little less traumatic,' Luciano commented tongue-in-cheek, reckoning that a few little treats like shopping trips round the fashion houses would quickly improve her attitude. Of course, he knew she wanted more and he was prepared to give her more to oil the wheels of persuasion. 'If you agree, I will naturally settle your debts here in the UK and compensate the men whose credit cards you stole so that they will drop the charges. That would remove the threat of arrest as well.'

In shock at that smoothly outlined proposition, Jemima snatched in a stark breath of astonishment and studied him with frowning eyes. 'But it wouldn't be right to let you pay those bills.'

Luciano raised a cynical brow. 'Of course you will be happy for me to settle your debts,' he countered forcefully. 'That is the sort of woman you are. Why are you trying to pretend otherwise?'

At that direct and unsettling question, Jemima flushed and hurriedly dropped her eyes. Julie would never have argued against such a benefit. In that he was quite correct. Her twin had always happily taken money to settle her problems and fulfil her dreams and not once had she protested or done anything that would have worked against her own natural interests. So, if Jemima was still set on pretending to be Julie, she had to bite her lip and go with the flow. She tried to take a sensible overview of her situation. The debts Julie had acquired in Jemima's name were a major source of worry to both her and her parents. To be free of that pressure would be wonderful, she acknowledged guiltily.

'And quite naturally *I* don't want my son's mother dragged into court over debts or dishonesty,' Luciano pointed out without hesitation.

But I'm *not* your son's mother, she suddenly wanted to tell him, because the web of her deceit was getting thicker and harder to justify. And what would happen if she simply told him the truth now? Would he still take her with them to Sicily? Still offer her the chance to learn how to part gently from the baby she loved? Jemima thought not. She stole a glance at him from below her lashes. She had *lied* to him. If he found that out, he would be so angry he would snatch up his son and walk away. He wasn't a forgiving or understanding or tolerant man. Furthermore the only thing she had to offer on his terms was that she was supposedly the mother of his son. Shorn of that borrowed status, she would have no standing whatsoever in his eyes.

'Obviously not,' Jemima conceded tightly before she could lose her nerve again. 'I'll come to Sicily with Nicky—'

'Niccolò,' Luciano corrected without hesitation.

'He'll always be Nicky to me,' she fielded quietly, refusing to give ground.

Something bright flashed in his dark gaze, lighting his eyes gold like the dawn sky, and she stiffened, like a small animal suddenly faced with a predator.

'Doing what I tell you to do would be a wise move now,' Luciano spelt out softly, his intent gaze raking down over the fullness of her pink lips, the swell of her tantalising breasts and the slim legs on view. He had never lusted after a woman of her ilk before. What did that say about him? But lust was healthy and indifference was not, he reasoned fiercely, all too reluctant to banish the sexual energy infusing him when for the first time in much longer than he cared to recall he felt *alive* again.

Suddenly restless, Jemima uncoiled her legs and stood up. 'You're trying to intimidate me.'

The golden gaze grew ever more intense. 'Am I?'

'I'll do everything that is reasonable but I won't be intimidated and I won't grovel,' she framed tautly, extraordinarily aware of the darker, deeper note in his rich drawl and the warning flare of his brows.

'You *won't*?' Luciano's intonation was soft and slippery as silk brushing her skin as he stalked closer, all predator, all threat.

And she should have backed away, she knew that was what she should do, but a current of inexplicable excitement was quivering up through Jemima and working its own seduction. 'I won't,' she confirmed shakily, her own voice dropping in volume and, to her annoyance, emerging breathily.

'But the idea of you grovelling at my knees is appealing, *piccolo mia*,' Luciano confided huskily, eyes golden and predatory as a raptor's locked to her upturned face. 'The image of you giving me pleasure while you're doing it gives me a high…'

At first, Jemima just couldn't credit that he had said that to her and then she told herself that he couldn't possibly have meant that sexual innuendo. A surge of embarrassment and uncertainty caused a burst of colour to fly into her cheeks and she blinked, trying to close him out, trying to rescue her brain from the sudden erotic imagery he had filled it with. That wasn't something that had ever happened to her before in a man's presence. She didn't imagine doing sexual things with men as a rule, but maybe if she had, a little voice whispered, Steven would not have been so stupefied by her infinitely bolder twin. Something about Luciano Vitale got to her on a primal level she had never experienced before.

'Did you really just say what I thought you said?' she mumbled unevenly.

CHAPTER FOUR

A HUSKY LAUGH escaped from Luciano. 'Is that how you work this spell with men who should know better? You flutter your lashes and blush at will and act naïve? Let's hit the bottom line and save some time. I don't *want* naïve or shy or fake virginal, Jemima. I like women who aren't afraid to be women…just as I am a man unafraid to admit when I feel like sex.'

Jemima was out of her depth and didn't know where to look or what to say. She couldn't admit that she wasn't a fake virgin and she couldn't admit to being naïve or shy when Julie hadn't had a shy or modest bone in her entire body. Julie had treated sexual invitations as ego boosts and had revelled unashamedly in male admiration. For just a moment, Jemima longed for the cool to emulate her late sister, who had taken her looks and sensuality for granted. *He felt like sex?* Involuntarily she glanced up at him again and a tiny little hot frisson ran up from her feminine core to pinch her nipples taut when she collided with his gleaming golden eyes. She felt the pull of his magnetic force then, the potent, compelling awareness of a powerful sexuality.

'And equally unafraid to act,' Luciano imparted, every predatory instinct in his big powerful body fired by her masquerade of innocence as he reached for her, determined to smash that façade that was so very foolish in the circumstances when he knew so much about her true character.

Jemima regained the strength to move a little too late, her paralysed legs moving her clumsily backwards in the unfamiliar room. He had knocked her off her usual calm, rational perch and wrecked her composure with that blunt sexual come-on. He had truly shocked her but he had excited her as well because, on a level Jemima didn't want to examine, she was hugely flattered by the idea that a male as gorgeous as Luciano Vitale could find her attractive.

As he spoke Luciano reached for her and propelled her back against the door she had almost reached, one hand closing round her shoulder, the other rising to curve to her chin. 'I like the chase. You're right about that, *piccolo mia*,' he told her incomprehensibly as if she had spoken. 'But this is the wrong time to run away.'

She was entrapped by his gaze, her chest swelling as she snatched in a needy breath, her throat tight with tension. Luciano Vitale wanted her. *Her?* The very concept turned her inside out because he was drop-dead beautiful in a way she had never dreamt existed. From the crown of his luxuriant black hair to his stunning eyes and flawless bone structure, he mesmerised her.

'Your pupils are dilated...' Luciano breathed, stroking a strand of golden hair back from her brow to tuck it below her ear, shifting closer, bending his dark head.

'Are they?' She was so insanely aware of how much taller and stronger he was, she was frozen with her hips welded against the solid wooden door. The lemony scent of his cologne assailed her nostrils. He smelled amazingly good and a ball of heat warmed in her pelvis.

'I scare you, don't I?' Luciano laughed again, startling her. 'I don't want to scare you...not any more.'

His breath fanned her cheek and she shivered, feeling the press of his long, powerful thighs and the hard, thrusting fullness at his groin against her stomach. Her whole body seemed to overheat at that point of contact. He was aroused and she had made him that way...she, Jemima Barber, without cosmetic witchery or fancy clothes. Who would ever have believed it? She felt like a real woman for the first time since Steven's betrayal. She didn't understand what possible appeal she could have for Luciano Vitale, but she didn't much care during that instant of exhilaration. As he lowered his head a little more and his lips brushed whisper soft across hers, it felt like *her* moment and it felt crazily like something she had been waiting for all her life.

Long fingers laced into her hair to hold her steady and the pressure deepened. She opened her mouth and he took immediate advantage with a dominance that thrilled rather than annoyed. His tongue darted into the moist interior and tangled with hers and she kissed him back with an eagerness she couldn't suppress. Her body took flight on new sensation, excitement rising like a tide inside her, drowning out every objecting voice in the back of her head. Every inch of her was suddenly tender and supersensitive, so that firm brush of his hand across her covered breasts made her straining nipples prickle in reaction and the trail of his fingers up her thigh as he lifted her skirt set her on fire with tingling impatience and longing. That passionate kiss held her utterly spellbound, her senses excited beyond bearing, and the throb of awakening between her thighs was almost unbearable in its intensity.

He stroked a fingertip across the tight triangle of fabric stretched between her legs and her knees turned to water. 'You're wet,' he told her thickly.

She couldn't breathe for shock at the tiny tremors of response quivering through her while the heat at the heart of her stoked higher. She had never in her life before wanted to be touched so badly and she was ashamed of the desire until his hungry mouth found hers again with bruising force and all thought fled in the same instant. One kiss and he dragged her under again while his skilled fingers strummed beneath her panties and stoked the hunger higher, sliding into the moist cleft and caressing the slick tissue before returning to the tiny bud that controlled her entire being.

She trembled and a strangled moan was wrenched from low in her throat as he rubbed her tormentingly sensitive flesh and suddenly her body was racing out of her control and she was jerking helplessly and gasping mindlessly beneath his mouth in a sudden explosive climax that blew her away. Her legs gave way and she would have fallen had he not lifted her and settled her down on the nearest seat.

Limp and shaking, she wrenched her rucked skirt down in a desperate movement. Shock was blasting through her and her heart was still racing. She couldn't believe what had just happened. She couldn't believe that she had let him do that to her...something so intimate, so inappropriate, so wanton...

'You were ready for that,' Luciano purred, staring down at her with smouldering dark golden eyes. 'You're a passionate woman.'

But Jemima had *never* been a passionate woman. Steven had told her that passion was for sluts and she had always been careful not to seem too keen in that line because that had seemed to be what he expected from her. When he had plunged into a wild fling with Julie she had been shattered at how quickly he had changed his attitude. Luciano, however, wanted that passion, *thrived* on it, she sensed in confusion, forcing herself to look at him, her face hot and flushed, her sated body still somehow feeling like a wanton stranger's.

'Let's not...talk about it,' she mumbled unsteadily.

'Let's not... I prefer to *do* rather than talk,' Luciano murmured, wondering why she was still acting so oddly. Touching her had been a mistake. He wanted more. Given the smallest encouragement he would have dragged her off to bed and eased the burn of his libido. He didn't want to wait. He wasn't used to waiting but he was suddenly very conscious of who she was. His son's mother. It would be most unwise to rock the boat before they reached the security of his Sicilian home, Castello del Drogo.

'It shouldn't have happened,' Jemima breathed tightly, rising from her seat and snatching up her bag. 'I don't know how it did—'

Luciano was not amused. 'It's simple. I wanted you. You wanted me—'

'I forgot where I was and who I was with for a moment,' Jemima corrected stiffly, still carefully evading his eyes. 'I was out of control.'

'I liked it.' Luciano could not understand why she was in retreat. With his knowledge of her, she should have been making the most of the situation and trying to please him. And he was very much in the mood to be pleased.

'You were talking about Sicily and…er…settling bills,' she reminded him stonily.

Ah, business first. He perfectly understood her change of focus. 'I will take care of them. You will have to sign a confidentiality agreement first. You will not be free to talk to anyone, and that includes the media, about the surrogacy agreement or about me or my son,' he informed her with forbidding cool.

'That's not a problem. I'll go and see if Nicky is awake yet. It'll be time for us to leave soon,' she said with scarcely concealed eagerness as she checked her watch.

Luciano stood watching the door swing shut on her exit. A black winged brow quirked. Was it some sort of a game she played with men? Give a little and then back off? Some men would want her all the more after that type of will-she-won't-she uncertainty. But Luciano was in no doubt that she would ultimately share his bed and her withdrawal irritated him. He hardened even more at the prospect of spreading those soft, rounded thighs and plunging between them until he had attained his pleasure. One night would probably be enough, he decided with a dark smile. He wanted her horizontal. For that single night he wanted her every which way up he could have her. That would work her back out of his system and possibly by that stage he would grasp what had attracted him in the first place.

At least there would be no complications with Jemima, he reflected as he phoned his housekeeper to make household arrangements. Never mind Jemima's little ploys, she knew the score. He would reward her richly for sex, for sharing physical pleasure without emotion or strings, and she would be quite happy to walk away again.

'I'm a close friend of Jemima's and her family,' Steven Warrington declared smugly as he walked into Luciano's office. 'And with respect, I'd like to know why you think it's necessary for her to accompany you and your child to Sicily.'

Luciano surveyed the smaller blond man with shrewd, unimpressed eyes. 'That's my personal business, Mr Warrington. But I see no reason not to tell you that my son is attached to Jemima and I'd like to minimise his sorrow when she moves on.'

'Taking Jemima to Sicily with you seems a strange

way of letting *her* move on,' Steven opined with another smile. 'I'd prefer it if you simply removed your
son now and left Jemima to get on with her life un-
encumbered.'

'Happily your opinion doesn't count,' Luciano fielded.

'It soon will. She's the woman I intend to marry.'

Luciano almost rolled his eyes at the idea of Jemima,
with her decided preference for the wilder side of life,
anchored by a wedding ring to the highly conservative male in front of him, but his lean, dark features
remained unrevealing. 'Congratulations,' he responded
smoothly.

The information he had already requested on Steven
Warrington was finally rolling up on Luciano's com-
puter screen as the younger man departed. Had Luciano
the patience, he would have received that information
before agreeing to see Warrington but curiosity had
driven Luciano to depart from his habitual caution.
So, Steven was an ex and there was a very, *very* long
list of exes in Jemima's chequered past. Did she leave
them all longing for a raunchy repeat? Although not the
ones whose wallets she had lifted, Luciano conceded,
while wondering why that aspect of her nature didn't
bother him more. She was a thief. Why did he want to
bed her? He had never knowingly wanted to bed a de-
ceitful woman before. Having grown up in the shadows of a crime-fuelled household, he was not drawn
to the dark side in any way. Unlike his late father he
was temperate and controlled.

Maybe he had been too ascetic in his habits for too
long, he reasoned in frustration, because he was still

struggling to understand the key to Jemima Barber's appeal. Even so, he wanted her and on those grounds he would have her simply because remarkably few things in life gave Luciano genuine pleasure. Steven Warrington's self-righteousness amused him. Jemima had no plans to marry Steven. He was quite sure of that.

But somehow that didn't eradicate an almost overwhelming temptation to smash a fist through Steven's blindingly white teeth. Luciano didn't comprehend the urge and he suppressed it, thoroughly off-balanced by that sudden lurch towards violence. He had felt it before, of course he had, with his very genes drenched in the violence and corruption of his forebears. But never ever had he had that experience where a woman was concerned and that awareness unsettled him. One night. He would have her in his bed for only one night, he assured himself grimly.

In any case, he reflected thoughtfully, it was not as though he could be at any real risk with Jemima, because Luciano didn't do emotional connections with anyone. His son would be the sole exception to that rule. Loving and caring for a child was pure and it wouldn't damage him or anybody else.

'I think it's the best solution for everybody,' Ellie declared bravely while Jemima was trying to console her weeping mother and her deeply troubled father as the four of them sat round the kitchen table over mugs of tea.

Jemima was feeling sick with shame at having hidden so much from her adoptive parents and she still did not feel up to the challenge of telling them the truth. They would have been horrified if they knew that she was pretending to be her dead sister and faking being Nicky's mother. No argument she could make would persuade them that such dishonesty was justified. In any case her parents were already dealing with quite enough. The older couple had returned from Devon only that morning to learn that their daughter and Nicky would be leaving the next day for a trip to Sicily, following which Jemima would be returning home *alone*. Unfortunately Julie's son had become as dear to Jemima's parents as any grandchild. They too had been part of Nicky's life almost from birth.

'Nicky is Luciano's son and the poor guy's been searching for him all these months,' Ellie pointed out, trying hard to support her friend's arguments in favour of the trip to Sicily and the inevitable surrendering of Nicky to his sole surviving parent.

'I believe he'll be a good father. He's only asking me along because he knows Nicky's attached to me and he doesn't want him to be hurt by me suddenly disappearing from his life,' Jemima explained afresh.

'Mr Vitale *is* being responsible,' her father conceded thoughtfully. 'Although I could never condone the agreement he made with Julie. That was rash and she was the worst possible candidate he could've chosen—'

'Yes, but don't forget it wasn't Julie he really picked. He believed he was picking Jemima.' Ellie was quick to remind the older man that Julie had applied to be a surrogate using her twin's identity rather than her own.

'True and you've certainly stood by the little chap,

giving him what he needs to flourish,' Jemima's father said to his daughter with warm approval. 'I suppose we'll simply have to wait until our daughter gives us a grandchild to fuss over, my dear,' he said to his wife.

Jemima paled beneath that look of approbation. She knew just how shocked her parents would be if they ever learned about the deceit she had employed in her dealings with Luciano.

That same morning, Charles Bennett made a return visit with a colleague in tow. He read through the confidentiality agreement with Jemima and explained every clause while his companion informed Jemima that he was there on her behalf to protect her interests. He spoke up on several occasions, pointing out that a lot of money could be made from selling stories to the media but that choosing to abide by Luciano's rules would be financially rewarded by a bonus once she had finished working for him. Jemima signed on the dotted line and was grateful when the lawyers left.

Later that same day, Ellie stood by grinning while Jemima patiently stood and obediently posed while all her measurements were taken and carefully noted down by the middle-aged female tailor and her assistant who had also called at Luciano's request.

'So, he's planning for you to wear a nanny uniform?' Ellie remarked teasingly after the women had departed.

Jemima pulled a face. 'Obviously,' she pointed out ruefully, far from looking forward to the prospect of being dressed in some starchy formal outfit in the Sicilian heat.

'I suppose it's one good way of ensuring that you

don't forget that you're one of the workers rather than a guest… I mean, it could be a bit awkward with you supposedly being Nicky's mother,' her friend opined with a wince. 'When are you planning to tell Luciano that you're Julie's sister?'

Jemima grimaced. 'Probably not until I'm leaving Sicily, which will be the end of August at the latest because term starts the following week and I'll be starting teaching again,' she reminded the other woman. 'It would be a bit of a risk admitting my true identity any sooner than that because Luciano could just ask me to leave immediately but by late August it's hardly going to matter to him.'

'Stop beating yourself up about it. You're not doing anyone any harm—'

'It's not that simple, Ellie. Every time I'm with Luciano I'm *lying* to him,' Jemima pointed out heavily, wishing she had found it possible to confide in Ellie about how much more complicated her relationship with Luciano had recently become. The problem was that she was too ashamed to admit that their strained relationship had suddenly—inexplicably, to her—dived into the kind of intimacy she had always held back from.

Only three days had passed since that day in London and she still lay in her bed at night unable to quite accept that she had fooled around with Luciano to the extent that she had forgotten not only the tenets that she had been raised by, but also everything she could not afford to forget about her current predicament. She was acting as Julie, not herself, and, although she

was convinced that her late sister would also have suc-
cumbed to the advances of a gorgeous billionaire, she
knew she couldn't grasp at that as an excuse for her
behaviour. In reality she had lost control and had allowed herself to be swept away on a roller coaster of
sexual sensation new to her. She had acted like a giddy
teenager rather than a grown-up, had lived in the moment, had *rejoiced* in the moment without any thought
of what it would be like to meet Luciano again or to
work for him in an official capacity.

'You're lying *solely* for Nicky's benefit,' Ellie told
her with loyal reassurance. 'And by going to Sicily
with Nicky you're making all these changes easier for
him—'

Jemima gave her friend an anxious look. 'So you
think I'm doing the right thing?'

'I always thought that the best solution for Nicky
was to be with the father who arranged for him to be
born. He's a lovely child, I can see that, but he's not
your child. I hate to agree with Steven about anything
but I do want you to get your own life back,' her friend
told her ruefully. 'Be young, free and single again. You
deserve that. Nicky was Julie's mistake.'

Jemima compressed her lips and said nothing. She
could not think of Nicky's bright, loving existence as
a mistake on any terms and being single and free had
proved a less fun-filled experience for her than she
had been led to expect. Nicky was part of her life now
and she loved him. She had not carried her nephew
through a pregnancy but the little boy felt as much a
part of her as though she had. She knew that walking

away from him was going to hurt her a lot, but, if that was truly what was best for Nicky in the long run, she would have to learn to live with that.

The next morning, Jemima, Nicky and their luggage were collected by a limousine accompanied by a car full of bodyguards. The trip to the airport was accomplished in record time and even boarding the private jet awaiting them was a fairly smooth and speedy experience. Jemima was surprised that Luciano was not on board and that, indeed, she and Nicky appeared to be the only passengers aside of the security staff, who took seats at the rear of the plane. The cabin crew made a big fuss of Nicky and were unceasingly attentive.

Luciano boarded in Paris, where he'd had a meeting, and the first thing he noticed was Jemima, curled up fast asleep in a reclining seat with Nicky out for the count beside her in his fancy travelling seat. Her mane of hair was braided when he wanted to see it loose again...even though he knew much of that hair was fake? He shook off that awkward question and scanned the worn jeans and casual washed-out top she sported with a frown of incomprehension forming between his dark brows. Why had she not yet made the effort to dress up for him...even once? No woman had ever been so sure of her hold on Luciano's interest that she would show up garbed almost as poorly as a homeless person! Or was this deliberate dressing down and this avoidance of glamour merely Jemima's highly effective way of ensuring that he bought her a new wardrobe?

Jemima wakened slowly, comfortably rested after having endured a final nervous, sleepless night in her parents' home. Luciano now sat across the aisle. Drowsily she studied his perfect profile, thinking that no man should have lashes that long, that dark or that lush or a nose and a jaw that would not have disgraced a Greek god. Butterflies found wings in her stomach and fluttered. Luciano turned his handsome dark head and she encountered dark golden eyes as lustrous as melting honey. A little quiver ran through her like a tightening piece of elastic, unleashing far less innocent responses that made her squirm with self-consciousness.

'We'll be landing in thirty minutes.'

'Right…er…I'll go and freshen up,' Jemima muttered, sliding out of her seat.

For a split second he gazed up at her, scanning the bloom of soft pink warming the porcelain complexion, which merely enhanced the ice-blue-diamond effect of her unusual eyes and the full softness of the lips he had already tasted. And his body reacted as instantly as a starving man facing a banquet, urgency and hunger combining in a mind-blowing storm of response. His strong jaw line clenching, Luciano gritted his even white teeth angrily and looked away, schooling himself to coldness again.

He didn't like losing control. He had never liked losing control. He had often seen his father lose his head in temper and living through the experience unscathed had been a challenge for everyone around him. Luciano had little fear that he himself would erupt into mindless violence, but he was absolutely convinced that reactions like passion and anger twisted a man's thinking processes and made bad decisions and human errors more likely. She would be in his bed this very night, he reminded himself soothingly. He would have what he wanted, what he increasingly felt he *needed* from her, and then this temporary insanity would be over and done with, decently laid to rest between the sheets. It astonished him, it even slightly unnerved him, that sexual desire could exercise that much power over him.

Jemima concentrated on the mechanics of feeding and changing Nicky while stubbornly denying herself the opportunity to look back in Luciano's direction. He was gorgeous and he had to know he was gorgeous. After all, he saw himself every time he shaved, she thought wildly. But that was not an excuse to stare and blush and act all silly like an adolescent who didn't know how to behave around a man. Absolutely not any sort of an excuse at all, Jemima reminded herself doggedly as she abstractedly admired how much Nicky's glossy black curls resembled his father's and resisted the urge to make another quite unnecessary visual comparison.

Suddenly the thought that she would be in Luciano's vicinity for the rest of the summer was a daunting one. She could never act polite and indifferent in the company of such a dynamic and passionate male. He lit her up like a fire inside but she ought to be fighting that tooth and nail. She was *lying* to Luciano and he was Nicky's father, which meant that there was no possibility of any normal relationship developing between them. Keeping her distance and resisting temptation were what she needed to do. Intellectually she knew that…but knowing and actually doing were two very different things, as she had already discovered. Unfortunately for her peace of mind, Luciano's attraction yanked at her on every possible level…

CHAPTER FIVE

LUCIANO'S PHONE BUZZED into life after they landed, shooting out a string of text messages and missed calls, every one of which hailed from his British lawyer, Charles Bennett. His mouth quirking as he wondered what could possibly have prompted the relaxed Charles to such an uncharacteristic display of urgency, Luciano phoned the older man as soon as he stepped inside the airport.

'I have the worst possible news for you. We've all been conned,' Charles announced with rare drama the instant the call connected. 'Jemima Barber is *not* the mother of your child—'

Luciano froze and waved an impatient hand at his bodyguards to silence their chatter while he listened. 'That's not possible,' he declared.

'I haven't got all the details yet and I won't waste your time with speculation but I believe that the mother of your child was one of an identical set of twins. She died when she was struck by a car a couple of months ago,' the lawyer explained curtly.

Luciano was frowning darkly. 'Which would mean—'

'That at best our Jemima is an aunt to the boy and

a con artist,' Charles framed drily. 'I have a top-flight set of investigators digging into this right now and I expect to have the whole story for you by this evening at the latest.'

'How sure are you of these facts?' Luciano prompted, watching Jemima detach his son's clinging fingers from her hanging golden braid. *Not* Niccolò's mother? How could that be? His brain, usually so fast to adapt to new scenarios, was for some reason still struggling to find solid ground in this shift of circumstances.

'Take it from me—she's definitely *not* the woman who gave birth to the boy. I now have that woman's real name along with a copy of her *death* certificate. She called herself Julie Marshall. Matters are complicated by the fact that from the very beginning of your dealings with Julie, your son's real mother was using Jemima Barber's identity to hide behind.'

'But why? You believe this was a conspiracy from the start?'

'Who can tell? With one of them dead it's doubtful that the full truth will ever be known,' Charles pointed out cynically.

Rage began to shadow Luciano's rational mind as the ramifications for his son began to filter into his thoughts. His son's mother had deceived him and his staff from day one and now she was dead and, as such, untouchable. Luciano was his son's only living relative. He refused to credit that an aunt could possibly have a claim to challenge his own. So, naturally, Jemima had not owned up to the truth. After all, her only way of making a profit through Niccolò was by *pretending* to be his birth mother.

As they climbed into a limousine outside the airport Luciano watched his son nestle trustingly into Jemima's arms and then complain loudly at being placed in the car seat instead. His lean dark features shadowed. He was finally a parent and already he had failed. He had failed to protect his son from hurt. Niccolò had been encouraged to form a bond with his two-faced, duplicitous aunt and would be emotionally bereft when the woman disappeared from his world. Who did Luciano blame for the formation of that deceptive bond? Jemima Barber! She must've known from the outset that her only weapon would be the baby's attachment to her. Niccolò was only a baby but he had already been tricked into bestowing affection where he should not. Luciano, in a rage beyond anything he had ever experienced, ground his even white teeth together while he pretended an interest in the emails on his tablet.

She was a lying, cheating *prostituta* with a stone for a heart! And just like her late sister, the only thing that greased the wheels in Jemima's world was money. There was no other explanation for her behaviour! At any time she could have admitted the truth but she had preferred to lie and stage a scam to ensure that she wielded the greatest power she could and made the biggest possible profit out of her dishonesty. In ignorance Luciano had agreed to settle her debts—her sister's debts?—and had made the mistake of offering her an all-expenses-paid trip to Sicily. And she would have even more cause to celebrate when she saw what awaited her at the castle...

Of course he didn't *want* her now, he told himself fiercely. He wanted nothing more to do with her and out of sight would be out of mind. How long had it been since a woman put one over on him? He suppressed a shudder of all too fresh recollection. What did it say about him that the women who most attracted him were thoroughly immoral and unscrupulous characters? Was that some hangover from his ancestral forebears? Something dark and shady in his blood that slyly influenced his choices?

Although Jemima was trying not to stare at Luciano she was convinced that something unpleasant had happened. She had watched his lean, darkly handsome face freeze into rigidity while he was talking on the phone at the airport. Had he received bad news? Some business setback? Or something of a more personal nature? Jemima acknowledged how very little she actually knew about Luciano Vitale. He was a widower who had lost a wife and a daughter and that was the summit of her information. But whatever was amiss, Luciano's jaw was rock hard with tension and he had barely acknowledged the existence of Jemima and his son since the jet had landed. Ironically, Nicky, who acted up whenever Luciano actively tried to get closer to him, now chose to stretch out an inviting hand towards his father, who might as well have been on another planet for all the interest he was showing in him. Still, there was yet another similarity between the two of them, Jemima reflected helplessly. Neither one of them could *bear* to be ignored…and ten to one that was exactly why Nicky was vying for attention now.

The limousine came to a halt and Jemima looked out of the window, surprised to see various aircraft parked. 'Where are we?' she asked.

'A private airfield. I use a helicopter to fly to my home,' Luciano divulged, his firmly modelled lips compressing.

Jemima's eyes widened in surprise. She had never been on a helicopter before and yet he evidently regularly used them just to travel home. Nothing could have more easily illustrated the vast gulf between their worlds. While they were boarding the helicopter, there was no further conversation, which was probably just as well because Jemima was concentrating on her exciting new experience.

As the helicopter took off Jemima peered out of the window to watch a slice of sea appear at a crazy angle. Her brow pleated in astonishment when the craft then flew out directly over the water. Where on earth were they going? Naturally she had assumed that Luciano's home was either in a city or in the mountainous interior but as the minutes passed on their seabound journey it was clear that their destination could only be another island.

She watched land appear again with keen interest. A bright patchwork of forested slopes, olive groves and a vast brown building on the shoreline of a long beach appeared. The building had towers and turrets like a castle, and as the helicopter dropped down to land in the manicured grounds enclosed by tall boundary walls she realised that it *was* a genuine castle.

'What's this place called?' she asked as she hopped down onto the grass and approached Luciano to take Nicky back off him.

'Castello del Drogo. The island is named for it. I'll keep him,' Luciano told her, hoisting the sleepy baby against his shoulder in a blatantly protective movement, his eyes as dark and cool as the night sky and about as far from melting honey as eyes could get, she thought ruefully.

Refusing to be quieted by his discouraging coldness, Jemima smiled. 'How long have you lived here?'

'A couple of years. It has the privacy I need. Intruders can only approach by sky or sea and both are monitored. I can walk by the sea here without fear of a camera appearing from the bushes,' he spelt out flatly.

They got into the beach buggy waiting to waft them up to the doors of the castle. Jemima was smiling, her earlier concerns forgotten as she rejoiced in the warmth of late afternoon and the beautiful gardens surrounding them. It would be really interesting to stay in a castle, she thought absently, studying the imposing fortress before her. 'How old is it?'

'The oldest section is medieval, the youngest eighteenth century.'

They mounted shallow steps to the giant porticoed entrance where two women awaited their arrival. Both wore black, one of possibly pensioner age and the other around fortyish.

The hall was an imposing oval shape with a marble

floor and black ebonised furniture inlaid with mother-of-pearl. Jemima was silenced by the sheer splendour of the castle, especially when she compared it to her parents' tiny retirement home. How could she ever have denied Nicky the wealthy lifestyle that his father evidently enjoyed?

'Do you own the whole island?' she whispered, unable to contain her curiosity.

'Yes,' he admitted in the sort of tone that implied that it was not a very big deal to own your own island, and in Jemima's mind the gulf between them stretched even wider.

Luciano introduced the older woman as his housekeeper, Agnese, and the younger as her daughter and Nicky's new nanny, Carlotta. He settled the baby into Carlotta's arms and addressed her in Italian. Jemima reminded herself doggedly of her agreement to step back from Nicky as he was borne off screaming, presumably to be fed and put to bed. As Carlotta mounted the stairs Jemima could hear her talking softly and soothingly to the distressed baby and her concern eased a little.

'Agnese will show you to your room,' Luciano announced.

Agnese's small creased face was as frozen as an ice sculpture. Telling herself that that was still preferable to a dirty look, Jemima followed the older woman upstairs and down a tiled passageway with ancient stone walls. Double doors were flung wide and light flooded across the most amazing bedroom Jemima had ever seen. Tall windows cast sunshine over the sumptuously hung four-poster bed. Gorgeous furniture vied with opulent fabric and a glorious floral arrangement to take her attention. Taken aback as she realised that the palatial room was for her use, Jemima hovered by the little table bearing the magnificent flowers and watched wide-eyed as an actual maid in a uniform appeared through one of the several additional doors to smile and stand back as though waiting to usher Jemima into the room she had vacated.

The housekeeper indicated with her hand that Jemima should take the invitation and Jemima obediently walked into a very large dressing room lined with built-in furniture. And that was when the show began. The maid began opening doors and rifling through hangers packed with garments to display them. Racks of shoes, drawers filled with silky lingerie and a dressing-table unit packed with cosmetics below a mirror surrounded by special lighting were duly shown off. Jemima's jaw dropped while she attempted to work out what all these items could possibly have to do with her. The maid passed her a tiny gift envelope and she slid out the card.

With my compliments, Luciano.

Jemima blinked and looked again, fingers tightening round the card as it slowly sank in on her that she had not been measured up for a nanny uniform as she had assumed but for a new wardrobe. She broke out in perspiration, her jeans uncomfortably warm. Luciano had given her a vast new wardrobe and as she flipped with anxious hands through the nearest selection she realised that it was all designer stuff, filled with famous fashion labels that even she, who didn't follow fashion, had heard of. She was gobsmacked, so gobsmacked that when the maid and the housekeeper departed she simply sank down on the boudoir chair by the dresser and stared back at her own unadorned face. Her face looked weird in the fancy lights, oddly bare and shocked, and she breathed in deep and stumbled upright to peel off her jeans before she could expire from heat exhaustion. In the bedroom she opened the suitcase she had travelled with and yanked out a cool cotton skirt to step into it.

But she still couldn't think straight. Indeed all she could think about was the contents of the dressing room. What on earth had she done to give Luciano the impression that such an extravagant gesture would be welcome? Her tummy gave a nauseous flip and she shut her eyes tight, hot colour burning her cheeks. Oh, yes, she knew what she had done. She hadn't said no when she should've. She hadn't said yes either, she reflected numbly. She had simply let him do what he wished. And evidently that had been sufficient to encourage Luciano to go out and spend thousands and thousands and thousands of pounds to enable her to dress like a queen. Hands cool now with shock, she pressed them to her hot cheeks and groaned out loud. My goodness, what was she going to do?

She was supposed to be Julie and Julie would have been ecstatic. Julie had adored clothes and everything her sister wore had carried a logo. Jemima blinked and wandered back into the dressing room. She trailed an uncertain hand across the soft smooth briefs still visible in an open drawer and sighed heavily. The clothing had been tailored to her exact height and size, but how could she wear it? How could she possibly say thank you and just wear it?

Neither a borrower nor a lender be and being wary of unexpected gifts was how Jemima had been raised. She also knew that old adage about being true to oneself. And accepting such largesse when she had done nothing to deserve it ran contrary to her principles. She swallowed back a heartfelt groan while she surveyed the racks of shoes. If Jemima had a weakness, it was for shoes and she swore her toes tingled like a water diviner's when she saw the cross-strapped green high heels studded with tiny twinkly stones. They called out to her feet and, kicking off her serviceable pumps, she slid her yearning toes into those tempting shoes. Yes, this was the way to be gracious, the only way not to throw all of Luciano's generosity back in his teeth; she would accept one small item to show gratitude. Having bolstered herself with that argument, Jemima tottered downstairs in her wholly inappropriate footwear.

Agnese was waiting for her like a little old witch in the hall.

'I'm looking for Luciano,' Jemima announced with a pleasant smile.

Agnese was eying the frivolous shoes with rampant censure. 'Il Capo is in the library.'

Il capo meant 'the boss', Jemima translated, having watched enough Godfather movies to recognise the lingo. Walking with precise but wobbling care in the direction of Agnese's pointing hand, Jemima wondered if the new wardrobe had given Agnese the wrong idea about the precise nature of Jemima's relationship with Luciano, and then she scolded herself for wondering, reckoning she had more to worry about than the suspicion that the staff had disliked her on sight.

Luciano had had four drinks in succession while he waited for Charles to call. His father had been a drinker and it was very rare for Luciano to drink to excess but his impatience to know the finer details of the scam was literally eating him alive. He couldn't wait to confront Jemima but he would not do it until he knew everything there was to know about her. He was *so* angry with her, so bemused by the strange conflict tearing at him. He was in turmoil and he didn't know why, which simply added another layer of hostile frustration to his mood.

Frowning at the sound of the knock on the library door, Luciano strode across the room to drag it open and discover who had dared to disturb him when he had requested peace. When he focused on Jemima's glowing, eagerly smiling face, he found himself taking a step back because he was initially surprised to see that she was happy. *But then she didn't know yet that he knew.* Of course she was happy, he ruminated bitterly, rage arrowing through him afresh. What else would she be but happy when he'd put her in a bedroom next door to his and given her a fortune in designer clothing? She was a gold-digger; naturally she was happy with her rewards. By bringing in Carlotta, he had even released

Jemima from the burden of constant childcare and very probably she was even happier about the prospect of greater freedom as well…

'Luciano…' she said softly and then her eyes flew off him to dart round the book-filled shelves. 'Oh, my, what a wonderful room! You are so lucky to have so much space for books,' she remarked chirpily.

'Is there a reason for your visit?' Luciano enquired forbiddingly, his attention clinging to her when she lurched a little on her path towards his desk at the centre of the room. His gaze skated down over her back view, lingering with pleasure on the ripe, rounded curve of her bottom shaped by the stretchy, clinging texture of the skirt she wore. His attention was then unwillingly caught by the colourful, glittery and ridiculously high-heeled shoes she wore below the skirt. For some reason she had teamed incongruous party shoes with her drab outfit and she could hardly walk in them, he registered in surprise as she clutched the side of his desk to steady herself.

Jemima studied Luciano and any hint of clear thought wilfully evaded her. No male that extraordinarily gorgeous could possibly encourage rational reflection in a woman, she conceded ruefully. He looked so tense and angry. His cheekbones were starkly defined, the line of his strong jaw rock hard. Yes, something had definitely gone wrong in his life. She was knocked sideways by the sudden realisation that just as Nicky's bad moods made her want to fix things for him, Luciano provoked the same need in her, only she didn't for one moment think that a cuddle and a soothing bottle would provide a magic cure for whatever ailed him.

Yet she still could not resist the temptation to offer. 'Can I help with whatever's wrong?'

'Why the hell would you think there's something wrong?' Luciano demanded harshly, hugely disconcerted by the question when in his experience other people couldn't read him at all well.

'Because there so obviously is,' Jemima pointed out, wishing he didn't have such stunning eyes. So dark and lustrous and sexy and absolute killers when fringed by black curling lashes into the bargain.

Unsettled by that assurance, Luciano gritted his teeth.

'You're so cross,' Jemima pointed out gently.

'I am not cross,' Luciano growled.

'I'll just mind my own business, then,' Jemima muttered, caving into the tension sparking like lightning rods through the atmosphere.

'Perhaps that would be best,' Luciano riposted very drily.

Her face flamed and she roamed restively over to the tall windows that overlooked flower beds surrounded by low box hedges and an ancient mossy fountain. 'I came down to speak to you about the new clothes you bought for me.' In emphasis she lifted a foot to show off the shoe she wore and very nearly fell over. All dignity abandoned, she grabbed at the back of an armchair to stay upright and hastily put that foot back on the floor. 'Er...these shoes are gorgeous... In fact it's all gorgeous, but with the possible exception of these shoes I can't possibly accept an entire wardrobe.'

'Why not?' Luciano shot back at her, startling her with that blunt comeback. 'And turn round and face me when you're speaking to me.'

With great reluctance and carefully slow movements, Jemima turned and straight away registered why she preferred talking to him without looking at him. Face on he was too much of a distraction. She lowered her lashes, blocking him out to some extent, her soft mouth unusually taut with nerves. 'Well, I'm very grateful for your generosity but I don't believe in accepting expensive gifts from people—'

'I'm not *people*!' Luciano cut in with ruthless bite. 'And I would hazard a guess that you have often accepted such gifts from men—'

'Yes…er…but that doesn't mean it was right. Having done it before, I don't have to keep on doing it,' Jemima pointed out, gathering steam in her argument. 'Maybe I think it's time for me to change my ways?'

'Maybe there are two blue moons in the sky,' Luciano incised with ringing derision.

'Being with Nicky *has* changed me,' Jemima argued, setting off on another tack. 'It's made me appreciate what's really important in life.'

'Within hours of his birth you had already decided what was really important to you…more money,' Luciano reminded her cruelly.

Jemima lifted her chin. 'But that doesn't mean I can't develop a different outlook. And I have changed. If you must know, I'm trying to turn over a new leaf.'

His dark eyes glittering like polished jet, Luciano vented a laugh of unholy amusement. 'I assume that's your idea of a joke…'

'No, it's not actually,' Jemima told him tightly, thinking sadly of the number of times her late twin had spoken of that same ambition to her. 'Everybody has to start somewhere when they make changes. I mean, why would you give me all those clothes anyway, for goodness' sake?'

'You're not that naïve.'

Her colour heightened. 'So, obviously it was a gift made with certain expectations, and if I'm not prepared to meet those expectations, I can't possibly accept it.'

'Of course you're prepared to meet my expectations.' Luciano surveyed her with galling assurance, smouldering dark golden eyes roaming over her with a potent sexuality that made her tremble. Her nipples prickled below her clothing and a tiny burst of heat ignited in her pelvis, starting up a nagging throb of awareness.

'I'm only here for a few weeks of summer for your son's benefit,' Jemima reminded him stubbornly. 'His benefit, *not* yours.'

Luciano said a rude word in English that made her flinch.

'I'm trying to be reasonable and honest here to avoid misunderstandings,' she told him in growing frustration.

Luciano stalked closer, silent and graceful as a night-time predator, and said an even ruder word in dismissal of that statement. What did such a woman know about honesty? What had she ever known?

He was so close now that Jemima could have reached out and touched him. Her heart was thudding out a staccato beat of apprehension and her breathing had ruptured into winded audible snatches.

She stiffened her spine and tilted her head to one side. 'I don't like your language.'

'I don't like what you're saying. I get very irritated when those around me talk nonsense or tell lies,' Luciano told her grittily, his Italian accent liquefying every vowel sound. 'You're trying to say that you don't want me and that is a *huge* lie!'

Her pale blue eyes widened. 'Are you always this sure of your own attraction?'

Long brown fingers lifted her braid from her shoulder and detached the tie on the end. He began to unlace the long golden strands. 'I want to see your hair loose…'

A new leaf, he was ruminating in disbelief. Could she really believe that he would be impressed by such drivel? How could she look at him with those luminous ice-blue eyes that seemed so candid and continue to lie and lie to his face? She was a completely shameless and stupid liar. Anger, bitter and jagged as a knife edge, cut through Luciano, burning and scarring wherever it touched. He was all too familiar with the cunning cleverness of female lies.

'This is getting too…too intense,' Jemima muttered uncertainly.

Luciano wound long fingers into the golden mane

of her hair to tug her closer. 'You shouldn't lie to me. If you knew how angry it makes me, you wouldn't do it.'

Her nostrils flared on the scent of him that close. Some expensive lemony cologne overlaid with clean, husky male and a faint hint of alcohol was assailing her and her tummy performed a nervous somersault. 'I'm going back home in just a few weeks,' she reminded him shakily. 'I'm only here for Nicky.'

'Liar...my son was not your primary motivation,' Luciano derided in a raw undertone, thoroughly fed up with her foolish pretences. 'You came here to be with me. Of course you did.'

Her brows pleated in dismay. 'Luciano...you're not listening to me—'

'Why would I listen when you're talking nonsense?' he demanded with sudden harshness.

Jemima looked up at him, scanning the dark golden eyes that inexplicably turned her insides to mush and made her knees boneless. As he lowered his head her breath caught in her throat and her pupils dilated. Without warning his arms went round her, possessive hands delving down her spine to splay across the ripe swell of her hips and haul her close. His mouth crashed down on hers with hungry force and in the space of a heartbeat she travelled from consternation to satisfaction. That kiss was what she really wanted, what her body mysteriously craved.

He kissed her and the world swam out of focus and her brain shut down and suppressed all the anxious thoughts that had been tormenting her. It was simultaneously everything she most wanted and everything she most feared. To be shot from ordinary planet earth into the dazzling orbit of passion and need by a single kiss was what she had always dreamt of finding in a man's arms, but Luciano was by no stretch of the imagination the male she had pictured in such a role. After all, Luciano wasn't for real. She might be inexperienced but she wasn't stupid and she knew that sex would only be a game with him and that he would only play with her without any intention of offering anything worthwhile. A woman needed a tough heart to play such games as an equal and she knew she wasn't up to that challenge.

'You want me,' Luciano grated against her red swollen mouth, his breath warming her cheek and bringing the faint scent of alcohol to her awareness.

Jemima shivered violently against the unyielding confines of his lean, muscular body. She loved the strength and hardness of his well-honed frame. Even through their clothes she could feel him hot and ready against her and the tight ache at the heart of her was like a strangling knot that yearned for freedom. The taste of his mouth was still on hers, nerve cells jangling with the longing for a repeat and the erotic plunge of his tongue. With a receptive shudder that signified the strength the gesture demanded, she brought up her hands and pressed against his broad chest to drive some space between them.

'No, not like this,' she mumbled gruffly, fighting herself as much as she was fighting his attraction.

She wanted him. He was right about that. She had never wanted anything or anybody as much as she wanted Luciano at that moment. Pulling free of him, stepping back, physically hurt as unsated cravings set up a drumbeat of angry dissatisfaction throughout her quivering body. Kicking off the silly shoes that limited her mobility was the work of seconds and her sudden loss of height disconcerted him into lifting his arms off her in surprise. Ducking out of reach and barefoot, Jemima darted round him and pelted out of the door as though baying hounds were chasing her.

Black brows pleating, Luciano swept up the abandoned shoes and looked at them incredulously. Did she think she was Cinderella or something? In bewilderment, because a woman had never before treated him to such stop-go tactics, he poured himself another stiff drink. He didn't get it. He really didn't understand why she was running away. Why would she do that? What possible benefit could she hope to attain by infuriating him?

And then the proverbial penny dropped and he wondered why he had not immediately grasped her strategy. After all, it was an exceedingly basic strategy: she wanted *more*. In fact Jemima or Julie or whatever she and her late twin had chosen to call themselves had been born wanting more. And she knew he was rich enough to deliver a *lot* more. Only he wouldn't, Luciano thought angrily, stoking up his resentment and his hostility. He was determined not to further reward a woman who had lied and schemed to make a profit out of his infant son as though he were a product on sale to the highest bidder.

CHAPTER SIX

BREATHLESS, JEMIMA LEANT back against the door she had slammed behind her in her haste to reach her bedroom. Well, so much for turning down the gift of the clothes with charm and diplomacy! Hadn't that gone well? She grimaced and groaned out loud. Why did she make such a mess of everything with Luciano? What happened to her brain? What happened to tact? Why had she kissed him back as though her life depended on it? Resisting him, acting repulsed would have kept him at bay, but instead she had encouraged him.

The trouble was, she thought ruefully, nobody had ever made her feel as Luciano Vitale did. When she was at college before she'd begun seeing Steven, plenty of men had tried to get her into bed. In fact being constantly badgered for sex had put her off dating. Ironically, though, she had not set out to still be virtually untouched at the age of almost twenty-four. Her parents might believe that she should remain a virgin until she married but Jemima had focused on a more attainable goal. She had believed that she would retain her virginity until she met someone she loved and she had believed she loved Steven, but Steven had seemed to prize her virginal state even more than her parents and had insisted that they should respect church teaching and wait until they were man and wife. Yet how quickly he had abandoned that conviction when true temptation had come along in the guise of her much sexier sister, she reflected wryly.

'You can't turn your back on true love,' Steven had told her self-righteously before he had gone off with her twin. 'Julie's the perfect woman for me.'

But Jemima couldn't tell herself the same thing about Luciano, not least because she didn't believe that he was perfect. He was arrogant and domineering and too rich and powerful for his own good. Yet she was madly, wildly and irrationally attracted to him. In addition she respected his sincere affection for Nicky. She also liked Luciano on a level she couldn't quite explain even to herself, for she did not know where that liking had come from or on what she based it. In the same way, when Luciano was angry and exasperated as he had been earlier she automatically wanted to make everything better for him and improve his mood. Why she felt like that she didn't know because common sense warned her that Luciano was wrong for her in every possible way. They were too different as people.

Sex was a pursuit in itself for Luciano, an amusement and not necessarily part of a meaningful relationship. Yet he *had* done commitment in the past. He had been married and a father before she'd even met him and at a relatively young age, Jemima reminded herself, and that suggested that while Luciano might have the reputation of being a womaniser he had always had a deeper and more caring side to his nature.

Across the room, a door opened and she glanced up. Luciano, his jacket and tie discarded, strolled towards her in his shirtsleeves.

'What on earth are you doing in here?' Jemima exclaimed in consternation.

'Finding you. You ran away,' Luciano condemned. 'Have you any idea how irritating that is?'

'You were being too pushy.'

'I'm naturally pushy.'

'That's not an acceptable excuse.'

'You were trying to pretend you don't want me,' Luciano reminded her with a sudden edge of accusation. 'That was an outright lie!'

'It's arrogant to be so full of yourself.'

Luciano shrugged a broad shoulder sheathed in smooth cotton. 'I'm not the modest type and I know when I'm wanted.'

And he would have had plenty of practice in that line, Jemima reckoned, scanning his lean, dark, flawless features and the intoxicating whole of his fallen angel beauty, which knocked her for six every time she looked at him. That was so superficial of her, she scolded herself, but when she was gazing at Luciano her brain could not concentrate on anything else. In any case her body hummed like an engine raring to go in his radius, making it difficult for her to breathe or move, never mind think.

'Perhaps you're waiting for me to offer you a villa or an apartment in Palermo or Rome or Paris…a less temporary and more rewarding position in my life?' Luciano suggested smooth as glass.

'Why would I want you to offer me a villa or an apartment?' Jemima asked him in genuine bewilderment.

'A mistress has some security. A casual lover has none,' Luciano pointed out.

'I really don't know what we're talking about here. I thought mistresses died out with corsets,' she confided jerkily, unnerved by the dialogue because he could not possibly be asking someone like her to be his mistress, his *kept* woman. That idea struck her as so ridiculous that a nervous giggle bubbled in the back of her throat.

'I don't want to talk,' Luciano breathed with sudden lancing impatience as he met her pale aquamarine gaze. He ran his hands through the thick tangle of hair tumbling round her shoulders. 'I like your hair. It's so long. Are you wearing extensions?'

'No, it's all me,' Jemima muttered breathlessly, because he was standing so close now that she could feel the heat of his body striking hers.

And right there, he knew he had her because he knew for a fact that only a few months earlier his son's mother had had short hair. But he had already accepted that she was a lying fake, hadn't he? Charles Bennett didn't make mistakes. Yet, trailing his fingertips through that lustrous skein of golden silk, Luciano couldn't have cared less about who Jemima was or what she was. He only wanted to see that marvellous hair spread across his pillows and without hesitation he bent and lifted her up.

'Put me down, Luciano!' she gasped.

'No,' he said simply. 'I want you.'

'That's not enough!'

Luciano shouldered open the door between their bedrooms. 'It's enough for me, *piccolo mia*.'

And she was on the brink of telling him why it wasn't enough for her when he kissed her, kissed her long and hard and hungrily until the blood drummed in her head and her toes curled and her mind went blank. Her fingers reached up and delved into his black curls, shaping his proud head, roaming down the back of his neck. The need to touch him was so powerful it overwhelmed every other prompting, even the cautious vibes trying to tug her back to sanity.

Luciano settled her down on his bed and studied her with immense satisfaction. He knew what she was. He knew what she was capable of. But he could not be damaged by a known threat. Her greed was a weakness he would use to control her, he reflected with satisfaction while only dimly questioning what had happened to his belief that one night would be sufficient for him. He knew he wasn't fully in control and it made him feel outrageously free of his rigid rules to do as he liked. She would be his for as long as he wanted her and that was all that currently mattered to him. He bent down and crushed her ripe mouth under his again, one hand closing to the rounded curve of her breast and feeling the race of her heartbeat. His own heartbeat was like thunder in his ears. Her mouth was hot and eager and sweet, so sweet that he couldn't get enough of it.

His kisses were like an addictive drug that Jemima

couldn't resist. Time and time again, she told herself, 'Just one more kiss.' And then what? a little voice piped up at the back of her head. Her spine arched as he lifted her and deftly released the catch on her bra. Before she could react he was peeling her top off over her head and tugging the bra down her arms.

'You're glorious,' Luciano husked, tracing her firm, full breasts with an almost reverent hand, pausing to toy with the protruding tips before bowing his head to lash his tongue across the tender crests.

Jemima huffed, lashes fluttering as sweet, seductive sensation snaked down from her nipples to her feminine core and joined the throbbing heat gathering there. Long brown fingers cradled her bare, rose-tipped curves and his mouth grew a little rougher while he teased the engorged buds, licking and suckling and nibbling with an erotic expertise that made her hips writhe against the mattress. She did not have a single thought in her head, only a sense of shock at the raw intensity of what he was making her feel.

With impatient hands he wrenched her out of her skirt and tossed his shirt on the floor to join it. Jemima gazed up at him with wondering appreciation, her attention lingering helplessly on the sleek bronzed torso composed of lean, hard muscle that swooped impressively down to frame a flat stomach and narrow hips. His shoulders were wide and as rounded with rippling muscles as his biceps. Only then as she reluctantly tore her attention from him did she become conscious of her naked breasts, but as she lifted her hands instinctively to cover herself he caught them in one of his and pinned them above her head.

'No interfering,' he told her in a roughened undertone. 'We only do this my way, *piccolo mia*.'

Colour washed her cheeks because she felt literally shameless lying there half-naked. He used his mouth to torment a straining nipple and she gasped, all self-consciousness wrested from her in the space of a moment. 'Let me touch you…' she pleaded.

He released her wrists. 'Some other time,' he mumbled, kissing a haphazard trail down over her ribcage and her tightening stomach to part her thighs.

Jemima froze, incredulous at his position and mortified, at least until he touched her and it was as if wildfire shot through her veins. Just as quickly there was nothing in her mind but a feverish concentration on what he was doing to her and how incredibly good it made her feel. Pushing her thighs back, he started slow with a long swipe of his tongue and when her hips lifted of their own accord he laughed softly.

'I'm really good at this,' he told her shamelessly.

And he didn't lie. He found every sensitive spot of arousal hidden in her tender folds, traced and teased those places with sleek, skilled fingertips, the glide and dip of his tongue and even the edge of his teeth. She could feel herself growing achingly wet in response, her heartbeat thumping inside her chest as if she were running a race. A fullness like a dam began to gather and build low in her pelvis and she turned this way and that to cope with the rise of heat and the throbbing torture of his electric exploration, restricted by his strong hold on her hips. Fire was burning through her as sensation piled on sensation at mesmerising speed. And then her own response started becoming more than she could contain, tiny spasms rippling through her quivering body and finally growing into a convulsive wave that swept her up and flung her high before sending her sobbing to earth again. She felt as though the top of her head were flying off while her body felt detached and heavy.

'I am burning for you, *piccolo mia*,' Luciano growled, sliding up over her to claim her mouth again.

He tasted of her and that shocked her but she was already in a state of shock so a little more didn't seem to matter. She had stepped out of her safe comfortable world into a far more dangerous one and learned weakness. And it wasn't the incredible allure of what he had made her feel that was her weakness, she acknowledged numbly. Her weakness was *him*. It was the heady joy she experienced when she saw the wicked smile in those lustrous golden eyes gazing down at her with satisfaction. It was knowing that his pleasing her had pleased him, made him feel good, lifted him out of the bad mood he had been in. That gave her a high more powerful than anything she had ever felt and incandescent warmth filled her.

'You do something crazy to me,' Luciano groaned as he rolled back from her to deftly take care of protection. 'I almost forgot to use a condom.'

Long fingers gripped her hips as he tilted her back and shifted against her. And she felt him nudge against her most tender flesh for the first time. It relit the fire that he had only recently sated, sending a frisson of reflexive hunger coursing through her again. Below his tousled black curls the arresting planes of his lean dark face were taut; his eyes blazed scorching gold with need. He took her mouth again with his, unexpectedly slow and gentle until his tongue delved between her lips and tangled with her own in a delicious dance. Nothing had ever been as arousing as that kiss and it fired her adrenaline. Her hands lifted to sink her fingers into his luxuriant hair and hold him to her but he pulled away a split second before he pushed into her.

'You're still so tight,' Luciano growled in frustration, stilling in an effort to accustom her to his girth, raw need driving his big powerful body as potently as a gun to his head.

She could feel her body stretching to accommodate him and apprehension gathered. She couldn't tell him that he would be her first because he believed she had birthed his son. He believed she was experienced and would undoubtedly prefer that to the rather pathetic truth. She squeezed her eyes tight shut and arched up to him in determined welcome, keen to get her introduction over with before the little regretful voices inside her head could gain her attention. And she knew what those little voices were about to tell her and she flatly refused to listen. She wanted Luciano and she wanted to know what all the fuss was about. His every tiny movement sent rippling sensation through her outrageously sensitive body.

Luciano pushed her back another few degrees to get a better angle and thrust home.

A searing flash of pain flared through Jemima and she cried out, eyes flying open filled with tears and surprise. 'That hurts!'

Luciano stilled, staring down at her with brooding, dark disbelief. He knew what his brain was telling him. He knew that his body had met with a resistance that he could not credit existed. While he had known she was not the mother of his son, he had certainly assumed she would be almost as practised with men as her sister had been. The awareness that he had got that badly wrong shook him back to full awareness, clearing his shrewd brain of the fog of alcohol and aggression that had clouded it.

'Are you OK?' he asked rawly.

'Yes, of course I am,' Jemima assured him and she shifted under him, washing wild sensation through Luciano's screamingly taut body while need continued to grip him like a hammer blow to the head. He eased out of the wonderfully tight grip of her and sank back into her with a groan of helpless satisfaction.

The pain diminished to a stinging discomfort closely followed by a jolt of exquisite pleasure. As Luciano moved the pleasure kicked in again and again and Jemima clutched at his arms, her knees rising as she arched to meet his next potent thrust. A wild singing impatience shot with primal need held her firmly in its grip and she lifted her hips in time to his fluid movements. He drove deeper and ground down on her and a helpless moan was torn from her lips as he picked up the pace. He slammed into her and her body clenched round him in excitement, her heartbeat thundering.

Glorious sensation shimmied through her pelvis and set up a chain reaction that sent her out of control when she convulsed beneath him. She plunged over the crest into a climax of intolerable excitement that sent spasms of delight rippling through her satiated body.

Weak as a kitten, Jemima wrapped her arms round Luciano only to stiffen as he literally shook her off. In a fluid movement he withdrew from her and sprang off the bed to stride into the bathroom. There was blood on him, Luciano acknowledged incredulously as he stepped into the shower. She had actually been a virgin. Where did that unexpected little attribute fit into the lying and gold-digging and plotting he had ascribed to her? What the hell had he been thinking? What the hell had he done?

Luciano pulled on jeans. Incredibly the mere thought of her lush, shapely body aroused him afresh and he wanted to punch something in frustration. A virgin? He was in deep shock and feeling ridiculously guilty. He had been so convinced that Jemima was a lying, gold-digging cheat like his son's true mother, *like…* No, he refused to go there, believing that the past was better left buried. But that past had made Luciano a cruel, distrustful cynic with women.

Jemima should have warned him. But how could she have without telling him the truth? Hadn't she appreciated that the first time might hurt? He had never had to think of that possibility before because he had never even come close to being any woman's first lover. He had been the first with Jemima, though, and he found himself savouring that knowledge in the weirdest way.

It shouldn't make any difference to his attitude to her...
but somehow it did. He could no longer confuse her
with Julie the escort or with his late wife, Gigi. Jemima
had been considerably more sexually innocent than
either.

Hearing Luciano's movements in the bathroom,
Jemima emerged from her own reverie and hurriedly
yanked the sheet up over her bare breasts even if the
gesture did strike her as too little too late. Luciano appeared in the doorway. What did he think of her now?
she wondered for a split second before reality finally
came crashing back down on her again. In the storm of
her personal doubts and insecurities she had miracu-
lously contrived to forget the lies she had told and they
were about to catch up with her, she reckoned wretchedly. Luciano knew now, he *had* to know that a virgin
couldn't possibly be Nicky's mum.

Where had her wits been when she'd let him sweep
her off to bed? How had she managed to overlook the
need to protect the one intimate fact that could prove
she was a liar? Of course it hadn't once occurred to
her that she would have sex with Luciano. Fantasy was
one thing, actually *acting* on fantasy something else
entirely. Nor had she calculated the very real danger
of tempting a male as aggressively dominant as Luciano. He was passionate and oversexed. Knowing she
wanted him, he had targeted her and she had been an
easy challenge, she reflected shamefacedly.

'So...' Luciano breathed silkily, leaning back against
the door frame barefoot and bare-chested, wearing only
well-worn jeans. With that much unclad masculine flesh

on view she found it impossible not to stare. 'What price do you put on your virginity?'

Jemima blinked. *'Price?'* she parroted in stricken disbelief.

Luciano raised a well-defined black brow. 'Well, obviously there has to be a price for me to pay because you put a price on absolutely everything else. You put a price on my son's worth, didn't you? Giving away something for free isn't your style.'

Her face had flamed hot as a fire. 'I don't know what you're talking about.'

Luciano shifted an impatient hand and studied her fixedly. 'Quit with the lies, Jemima. Lies only make me angry and you don't want me angry,' he warned her.

Lean muscles flexed below bronzed skin as he changed position. The deep chill in his assurance crept through her like the sudden touch of icicles on too-hot skin. He was scaring her but he didn't need to scare her because Jemima was already fully aware of the wrong she had done. 'All right, I won't tell you any more lies,' she muttered heavily. 'You know I'm not Nicky's birth mother now, don't you?'

'Obviously. So what's the going rate for a virgin these days?' Luciano asked with scorching derision. 'Presumably you gave it up for a good reason and with you the reason will always relate to profit.'

'I'm not like that, Luciano!' Jemima exclaimed in consternation.

His beautiful sensual mouth twisted. 'If you can try to sell a baby, I assume you can put a price tag on virginity.'

'I wouldn't ever have tried to sell a baby!' Jemima argued fiercely. 'I know how wrong that would be!'

'But it wasn't wrong to keep his father from him when his mother was already dead?' he shot at her smoothly.

Jemima flinched at that direct question, sudden tears springing to her eyes and stinging like mad. She could not even blame her late twin for her predicament. Indeed she was all too well aware that she had buried herself in the hole she had dug. After all, *she* had lied to Luciano from the moment she'd met him and compounded her errors by having sex with him. She had done worse than blur the boundaries between right and wrong, she had stepped right over those boundaries.

'My first question should be...*who are you*?' Luciano drawled. 'But then that would make me a liar too because I already knew that you weren't who you were pretending to be before we hit the bed.'

Jemima stared at him in dismay. 'You already knew?' she exclaimed, disconcerted yet again. 'And yet you *still*...' Her voice drained away as she glanced involuntarily at the disordered bedding.

Angry tension pulled Luciano's muscles taut. 'I wasn't expecting a virgin...'

Jemima was still struggling to accept his earlier statement. 'You knew I wasn't Nicky's mother and yet you were still willing—'

'Sex is sex, Jemima, and I had had a lot to drink. When the urge controlled me, I didn't really care who you were,' Luciano told her with derision.

Her tightly controlled face washed pink and then ran pale. She knew she was being punished for not being more careful about who she became intimate with. He was telling her that he had just used her to scratch an itch and that the shock of her true identity hadn't been enough to repel him. 'How long have you known?' she whispered sickly.

'Since we landed in Sicily.'

Her pale eyes widened because she was recalling his change of mood at the airport. 'I know what you must think of me—'

'You have no idea what I think of you,' Luciano cut in with icy bite.

'I love Nicky so much—'

'Of course you're going to say that.'

'I was afraid that if I told you I was only his aunt, you'd just take him away immediately.'

'I expected you to say that too,' Luciano incised, lounging back against the door frame, the light behind him glimmering over his powerful pectorals and the hard slab of rippling muscle below.

'I've been with Nicky since he was only a few days old,' Jemima told him in her own defence while struggling not to sound pleading.

'And you knew all along that your twin had acted as a surrogate mother?'

'Yes, but she wouldn't tell me your name or any details. Julie didn't trust anyone...*ever*,' Jemima completed with feeling emphasis. 'She knew that I wasn't comfortable with the decisions she had made and although she left Nicky in my care she didn't give me any information that I could have used to interfere with her plans.'

Luciano wasn't convinced. Consistent liars told more lies with ease, adding complex layers of falsehood to their stories to make them seem more credible. Been there, done that…visited the graves, he conceded with a sudden deep inner chill of recoil from his own experiences. His dark eyes iced over with a diamond glitter.

'You and your sister grew up in separate adoptive homes?'

'Yes…'

'And when did you first meet her?'

'A couple of months before she got involved in the surrogacy agreement with you and she didn't tell me about that until she turned up again with Nicky.' Jemima dragged her attention from him to study her tightly linked hands. Time was flinging her back almost two years and reminding her of her excitement and joy when she had first discovered that she had a twin sister who wanted to meet up with her.

Jemima had not tried to trace her birth parents because she had been fearful of hurting her adoptive family's feelings. It had not, however, occurred to her that she might have a sibling to find and she had been overwhelmed by Julie's first approach. It had hurt to learn that her birth father was unknown and that their birth mother had died from drug addiction, but it had hurt more to hear about her twin's early health problems, her unsuccessful adoption and unhappy childhood.

'I was so much more fortunate than Julie was. My parents loved me from the beginning,' Jemima said tautly. 'It wouldn't have mattered if I'd been a bit slow at school but Julie's family—'

'I'm not interested in Julie's life story,' Luciano cut in smoothly.

'She's Nicky's mother!' Jemima condemned.

'And I'm grateful she's not here to cause my son any more damage,' Luciano told her truthfully.

'That's an appalling thing to say!' Jemima slammed back at him, sliding her legs off the bed and yanking violently at the sheet for cover.

'Is it?' Luciano rebutted grimly, angry dark eyes hard as obsidian. 'She was his mother and that gave her rights over him but she wasn't a decent, caring person fit to exercise those rights!'

With a final forceful jerk, Jemima dislodged the sheet and wrapped it round her naked body to stalk back through the interconnecting door into her own room. Eyes wet with tears, she was trembling. Her first foray into sex had gone badly wrong and made her feel worthless and rejected. Her late sister was being abused and there was very little she could say because Julie *had* done wrong. But very few people were *all* bad. Jemima blinked back the tears as she dug through her case to extract her dressing gown and dropped the sheet to walk into the bathroom.

She needed to shower, wash away the memory of Luciano's touch and the feel of his body on hers. Shivering, she switched on the water. Her mind drifted back inexorably to her sister and powerful regret filled her because she kept on thinking that if she had only had a little more time with Julie she could have got closer to her and somehow changed things for the better. On another, more rational level, though, she was painfully aware that Julie had never listened to her and had neither respected her opinion nor sought her advice, particularly where Nicky had been concerned.

But Nicky had crept into his aunt's heart the moment she'd met him because he had been a most unhappy baby.

'I don't know how to be a mum!' Julie had complained, becoming almost hysterical because her son had been crying and inconsolable. 'You tell me to cuddle him but I don't feel comfortable with that. He's making *me* feel bad!'

Nicky had suffered from colic and Julie had not been able to cope with him or the sleepless nights. Jemima had tried to help and had ended up taking over. She had blamed herself when Julie had gone back to London to work, leaving her baby in Jemima's care. She had blamed herself too when her twin had failed to bond with her child but she had also been aware of Julie's chequered past history. In truth Julie had had many troubled relationships in her life and rarely settled anywhere for any length of time. Running away from difficult situations had been the norm for Julie.

Luciano had no compassion, Jemima thought wretchedly. Julie had done bad things but her sister had not set out to be a bad person. Tightening the tie on her dressing gown, Jemima walked back to the door that still lay open between the two bedrooms.

'I loved my sister…and I won't say sorry for that!'

Jemima told Luciano defiantly. 'But I *am* sorry I lied to you. That was wrong. I got too attached to Nicky and I was frightened of losing him but I do appreciate that that doesn't excuse my not immediately telling you that his mother had passed away.'

Luciano's full sensual mouth twisted. 'It was a power play, wasn't it?'

Jemima gazed back at him without comprehension. 'Power didn't come into it…'

Somewhere in the distance she heard a thin high-pitched wail and stiffened. 'Nicky's crying,' she muttered, walking to the door.

'Carlotta will take care of him,' Luciano countered.

Wrenching open the door, Jemima listened to the wails drifting down from the floor above and started down the corridor. 'I can't leave him upset,' she called apologetically over her shoulder, sensing Luciano's disapproval and refusing to look back at him.

She would be gone from his fancy island castle soon enough, she reflected wretchedly. He was hardly likely to allow her to stay now that he knew she had lied to him and had no real claim to Nicky. Yet it still stunned her that he had gone to bed with her in spite of that knowledge. He had admitted that he had been drinking. Inwardly she cringed. Had alcohol made her seem more attractive than she was? Why was she even thinking in such a way? What did it matter now? They had had sex and there was no going back from that. It had been a casual thing for him and he had been quick to vacate the bed afterwards. He had actually asked her what price she put on her virginity, she recalled painfully. She felt ashamed and humiliated and blamed him for it.

Why, oh, why had he had to make her feel so bad about their ill-starred intimacy?

CHAPTER SEVEN

CARLOTTA WAS ANXIOUSLY rocking Nicky in her arms. His little face was scarlet with tears and he was sobbing noisily.

'He doesn't like being rocked when he's upset,' Jemima told the brunette in an apologetic tone, thinking that it would have made more sense if she had been given the opportunity to consult with the nanny *before* the other woman started taking care of Nicky.

A voice spoke up in Italian from the doorway and Carlotta gave Jemima a frowning look of surprise before turning rather abruptly to hand Nicky over to her. Although conscious that Luciano was present and had acted as an interpreter, Jemima ignored him and concentrated on his son. Nicky went rigid as he was passed over and then sagged against her, shoving his face into the curve of her neck and whimpering.

'He has nightmares. He's frightened when he wakes up. He only needs to be soothed,' Jemima declared, walking the floor of the elaborately decorated room with Nicky cradled in her arms. She was still alarmingly conscious of the ache at the heart of her body and hot pink flushed her cheeks as she buried her face in Nicky's tumbled curls, revelling in the clean baby scent of innocence. With a heavy sigh she sank down into the rocking chair beside the cot.

Luciano had paused long enough to grab up a shirt and don it on his way to the nursery, but nobody seeing his bare feet and rumpled damp hair could doubt that he had recently undressed only to get dressed again in a hurry. Naked below her sensible dressing gown, Jemima could feel her face burning as if she were on fire. Their mutual state of undress was noticeable and embarrassing. She didn't want anyone to know or guess that she had slept with Luciano. That was her private disgrace and not for public sharing. Carlotta, however, simply smiled at Jemima, clearly relieved that the baby had calmed down.

His son's sobs had subsided almost immediately, Luciano registered without surprise while he watched. The baby's fingers clutched convulsively at Jemima for reassurance. Niccolò had missed her. Obviously he had missed her. How much of the little boy's misery had been caused by the sudden change in his routine and surroundings and the equally sudden absence of the one person he trusted? Luciano paled beneath his dark skin, shaken by the reality that he had set down rules that could well have hurt his son and caused him unnecessary suffering. He had instructed Carlotta to deal with the baby alone and to involve Jemima as little as possible in his care.

But how could he love his son and yet deny the child the one person whom he so clearly loved and wanted?

Shame writhed inside Luciano, a reaction he had not experienced in more years than he cared to count. He watched her smooth the baby's head with a tender hand and read the softness in her eyes.

'He knows his mother,' Carlotta said quietly in Italian to her employer.

It seemed a terrible irony to Luciano at that moment that Jemima was *not* his son's mother because the boy was deeply attached to her and she was equally attached to him. He realised he needed to talk to his lawyer to find out exactly what kind of woman Jemima Barber was. How could he trust his own instincts now? Nor could he have any faith in what Jemima's version of the truth might be. Anyone determined to speak up in defence of Julie Marshall would have failed to inspire Luciano with confidence.

As he stepped unconsciously closer to the woman in the rocking chair Nicky lifted his head off Jemima's shoulder and stared at Luciano with wide dark eyes. And then he smiled with sudden brilliance, freezing his father to the spot in shock for it was the very first positive response Luciano had received from his son. It was significant too that the child had smiled only when he was secure in Jemima's presence, he acknowledged ruefully.

Resting his head back down drowsily again, Nicky fell asleep. Getting to her feet, Jemima lowered him with care into the cot, straightened his sleep suit and covered him up gently. 'He should sleep the rest of the night now,' she whispered.

Luciano stared down at his slumbering son, then

glanced up again and noticed that Jemima was deliberately avoiding looking at him. Annoyance skimmed along the edges of his sensitised awareness as they left the room. She tried to step past him out in the corridor but he rested a staying hand on her arm.

'Jemima...we—'

'I'm really hungry,' Jemima proclaimed in a rush, jerking her arm back out of reach and addressing his shirt-clad chest. 'Would it be too much trouble for me to have something to eat in my room? Even a sandwich and a cup of tea would do.'

'Put on something in your new wardrobe and come downstairs to join me for dinner instead,' Luciano suggested, falling into step beside her as she walked down the corridor.

Her facial muscles clenched tight. 'Thanks but no, thanks... I'm not in a very sociable mood.'

As she descended the stairs she saw a huge portrait of an exquisite brunette on the landing and, already regretting her tart reply to his invitation, she said in an effort to break the pounding silence, 'My goodness, who's that?'

'My mother, Ambra. It was painted shortly before she married my father. She probably never smiled like that again,' Luciano breathed harshly.

His intonation made Jemima wince. 'When did she die?'

'When I was three years old,' Luciano admitted between gritted teeth, fighting off his terrible memories with all his might.

'Did your father remarry?'

'No.'

Jemima was already scolding herself for surrendering to her low mood and turning down the dinner invite. She had allowed Luciano to believe that she was the surrogate mother of his son and had used that pretence as a means of staying in Nicky's life. Was it any wonder that he despised her? Or that he had assumed that she was like her sister and after his money? Julie had worshipped rich men and money. Yet no matter how much money Julie had had it had never been enough and money had trickled through her fingers like water.

'We'll talk over breakfast in the morning,' Luciano breathed in a driven undertone as he came to a halt outside his bedroom door, which was mere feet from hers.

'I shouldn't have lied to you,' Jemima began, and then an unfamiliar stab of angry bitterness powered through her regret and she added, 'But you had no right to insult me by suggesting that I would use sex as a means of making money!'

Luciano ground his teeth together and watched her long, unbound mane of golden hair slide off her shoulders and fall almost to her waist as she moved her head. He wanted to run his fingers through that glossy golden hair so badly that he clenched his hand into a fist to restrain himself. So, he liked the long hair? OK, he really, *really* liked the long hair, particularly now that he suspected it was one hundred per cent natural. He also liked her body…and her eyes…and… With a huge effort he focused on what she had said and murmured grimly, 'I've met a lot of women who sell sex like a product.'

Jemima was so shocked by that blunt admission that she turned up her head to stare at him, ice-blue eyes visibly dismayed. 'Seriously?'

Teeth gritted more than ever at such naivety, Luciano nodded and wished he'd kept his mouth shut. Now she was probably thinking that he consorted with hookers and he didn't want her thinking that. *What the hell does it matter what she thinks?* he snarled at himself, thoroughly disconcerted by his loss of concentration and self-discipline. What was wrong with him? Had the few drinks he had imbibed in his bad mood completely addled his brain? Telling Agnese to hold dinner, he strode downstairs to call his lawyer.

Charles did a great deal of groaning and apologising during the lengthy exchange that followed. Nothing about the situation was quite as anyone had assumed or as clear. Charles still couldn't answer all his employer's questions and reluctantly gave Luciano the phone number of his own chief informant. Breathing in deep, Luciano telephoned Jemima's adoptive father, Benjamin Barber. And not one thing that Luciano learned in the subsequent conversation made him feel happier. Instead he came off that call marvelling at the older man's optimistic and forgiving outlook while feeling a great deal worse about his own opinions, suspicions and activities. Knowing that the least he owed Jemima was a polite warning about what he had done, he mounted the stairs again and knocked on her bedroom door.

Half asleep after her delicious meal, Jemima rolled off the bed and lifted her tray, assuming someone was calling back to collect it. Instead she was faced with Luciano, infuriatingly immaculate again in tailored chinos and a black tee shirt. 'Yes?' she said discouragingly, clutching the tray and feeling horribly irritated that she had not known it would be him at her door.

He leant down and took the tray, setting it down on the table to the side of the door. 'I have something to tell you—'

'Can't it wait until breakfast time?'

'I'm afraid not.' Soft pink mouth compressed, Jemima grudgingly stood back to allow him into her room. Since she had no idea what he had to say to her, keeping him out in the corridor where their conversation could be overheard struck her as risky.

'I spoke to your father an hour ago and we talked for quite some time.'

Transfixed by that staggering announcement, Jemima stared back at him in horror. 'I beg your pardon?'

'I phoned your father and he's now aware that you were pretending to be your sister for my benefit,' Luciano divulged.

'Oh, my goodness…how could you *do* that?' Jemima was aghast at the news. 'I just can't believe you told him!'

'The investigators my lawyer employed had already contacted him and it made sense for me to address my questions to your father direct. He was troubled that you hadn't told him what you were doing but he understands why you did what you did and he wants you to know that he forgives you. I had to warn you in case you were planning to phone home.'

Knees weakening, Jemima sank down on the foot of the bed and bowed her head into her raised hands. 'I can't believe you approached Dad… I've tried so hard to keep my parents out of all this!' she exclaimed reproachfully.

'I wanted a clearer picture of what happened and you're too emotionally involved,' Luciano drawled in self-defence. 'It was…enlightening to hear the facts from your father's point of view.'

'I hate you!' Jemima flung at him furiously. 'You had no right to go snooping and interfering!'

'I'm as trapped in the mess your sister left behind her as you are,' Luciano contradicted coolly. 'The legal ramifications of her having stolen your identity will take a long time to unravel. She gave birth to a child using your name. She contracted debts in your name and she broke the law using your name—'

Jemima flew upright in one tempestuous movement. 'Do you think I don't know all that?'

'She took advantage of you and your parents,' Luciano delivered grimly.

'There's no way my father said that!' Jemima accused furiously.

'Your father is a rather unworldly man and I imagine he has had little contact with the criminal element. I'm rather less innocent and much more accustomed to dealing with life's users and abusers.'

'Bully for you!' Jemima snapped back childishly, marching back to her bedroom door and dragging it open in invitation. 'Right now all I want to do is go to bed and forget you ever existed!'

Luciano lifted his hand and a forefinger flicked the full tense line of her lower lip in reproof. 'What a little liar you can be. Without me there would be no Niccolò…and somehow I don't think you'd give him up so easily.'

The touch of his hand against her lip made her entire skin surface tingle. Her breathing quickened and she pressed her thighs together to suppress the tiny clenching liquid sensation low in her pelvis. Her lashes swept up fully to collide with stunning dark golden eyes welded to her every move and change of expression. Her cheeks coloured, her lashes swept down and she backed away from him, furious that without even trying he could still get a physical reaction out of her.

'Goodnight,' she said flatly.

Luciano wanted to scoop her up and carry her back to his bed. It was pure lust, he told himself furiously, the sort of irrational, ungovernable lust that sent a man into cold showers and the depths of neurotic desire. And unlike his late and unlamented father, who had once become obsessed with a woman, Luciano was not the obsessive type. He stayed up late working and by the time he finally fell into bed he was too exhausted to do anything but sleep.

The next morning, Jemima felt more like herself and less traumatised. The truth had come out and she couldn't hide from it. Lying had gone against her nature and weighted her conscience and she was relieved not to be pretending any more. Her parents knew. She chewed her lower lip and decided to phone home that evening, although she dreaded dealing with her father's disappointment in her behaviour. Luciano and Nicky, however, were an even bigger challenge.

Presumably over breakfast Luciano would tell her what he wanted to do next and when she would be flying home. She had lied to him. She might have convinced herself that she had lied for her nephew's sake but in her heart she knew she was lying to herself. In reality, she had not been able to face parting with Nicky and that had been selfish when Nicky's father was available to take charge of his son. While she thought unhappily about her mistakes, she rooted through her suitcase, grimacing at the reality that there was really nothing in her case suitable for a hot day. At least nothing presentable, she affixed ruefully, choosing not to examine why what she wore had to be *more* presentable than usual when Luciano was around. After a few moments, she stalked into the dressing room and skimmed through the hanging dresses. What would he do with them after she had gone? Chuck them out? Pass them on to staff or recycling? She lifted down a fitted blue cotton sundress, plainer in style and less revealing than most of the other garments, and began to get ready.

Seated on the floor in the nursery, Nicky was happily playing with his new toys. Carlotta was friendly, addressing Jemima in broken English to let her know that he had slept well and eaten. A maid met Jemima at the foot of the stairs to show her where she was to go to join Luciano. They trekked across the vast building, mounting stairs and crossing hallways before walking down a long picture gallery that opened to an outdoor area that overlooked the sea and the shore.

The panoramic view and the sunlight blinded her and she had a split-second sizzling snapshot of Luciano, rising with fluid grace from his seat, his lean, powerful body sheathed in an exquisitely cut pale grey suit teamed with a black shirt. *'Buon giorno,'* he murmured smoothly. 'You look amazing.'

Jemima flushed. 'Let's not get carried away,' she told him reprovingly. 'I'm wearing this because it's so hot and I have nothing suitable *and*—'

'Rest assured I will not assume that you are wearing it either to please or attract me, *piccolo mia,*' Luciano incised as drily as though he could read her mind.

Her flushed cheeks turned a solid mortified red and she averted her eyes as she dropped down hurriedly into a seat. Dishes were proffered by one manservant, beverages by another. Her attention briefly falling on the bodyguards standing several yards away, it occurred to her that Luciano lived rather like a king in a medieval court with an army of staff and everyone bowing and scraping and doing their utmost to ensure his protection and his comfort. It was an isolated lifestyle, divorced from normality, and she wondered how it would affect Nicky to grow up like a crown prince in the lap of such indescribable luxury.

From below her lashes she stole a helpless glance at Luciano. He was looking out to sea, his flawless classic profile turned to her. Her heart thumped very loudly in her ears because she was remembering his mouth, that wide, sensually skilled mouth, roaming over her and making her writhe with raw need and then the dynamic flex and flow of his lithe body over hers, driving her to the apex of excitement. Perspiration broke out on her skin and she quickly looked away from him again. No, try as she might to be sensible, she could not forget the intimacy, the first she had ever known and, much like Luciano, utterly unforgettable.

'So, what next?' she muttered in the pulsing silence.

Lustrous dark golden eyes ensnared hers and her breath tripped in her throat. 'That's what we have to decide.'

Jemima tore her eyes free and bit into her fresh fruit. He was using the royal 'we'; she didn't think she would have much actual input into what happened next.

'Tell me how your sister got hold of your passport,' he invited, startling her with that request.

'It happened by accident. The first time we met she showed me her passport because she had worn her hair long then too, and I got out mine and we were laughing and somehow our passports got mixed up.'

'And?' Luciano prompted.

'Julie only realised she had my passport when she was flying out to Italy and she travelled on it because she didn't want to miss her flight.'

'She lied,' Luciano murmured without any expression at all. 'She had already used *your* passport in her application to be the surrogate I hired. And the reason she lied was that she had several criminal convictions in her own name. She probably tracked you down quite deliberately. She set you up to steal your identity, Jemima. Accept that.'

Jemima paled. She was remembering laughing with her sister as they compared unflattering passport photos. 'It was months before I found out about the…er… exchange and when I contacted her about it, she said she'd give it back when she returned from Italy.'

'Only she never did,' Luciano completed.

'Obviously you think I'm very stupid,' Jemima said tartly, burning her mouth on an unwary sip of coffee and swallowing hard, burning her throat into the bargain, tears starting into her eyes at the discomfort.

'No, I think you were scammed. She was a practised, confident trickster and she was your sister and you didn't want to accept the truth,' Luciano said in a surprisingly uncritical tone. 'I can understand ignoring the evidence and wanting to believe the best of someone close to you. It happened to me once.'

'Oh…' Jemima was taken aback by that admission. 'I loved her—I felt an immediate sense of connection with her.'

'Scammers have to be attractive to pull people in.'

Jemima concentrated her attention warily on eating.

'Why didn't you go to the police about your passport when she refused to give it back?'

'I didn't need my passport because I couldn't afford to travel at the time…and I didn't want to get her into trouble. For a long time she made excuses about why she wasn't returning it and I believed her,' she admitted with a rueful roll of her eyes.

A manservant topped up Luciano's black coffee. He rose lithely from his seat and lounged back against the stone balustrade girding the terrace. He surveyed her with satisfaction. She was elegant as a swan in the tailored blue sundress, her hair restrained in its usual braid, only stray little golden hairs catching the slight breeze round her troubled face. She had loved and cared for her sister, contriving to mourn Julie Marshall's passing in spite of all the damage her sibling had done. Jemima had a lot of heart and a generosity of spirit that he admired even though he couldn't emulate it. And he wanted what she had to offer for his son. He sensed that she could be the greatest gift he would ever give him.

For once he wasn't going to be selfish and he wasn't going to remind himself how often he had sworn never to surrender his freedom again. In any case he owed Jemima a debt. In the grip of ignorance and lacerating bitterness at her betrayal of trust he had seduced her and she hadn't deserved that. Virginity had to matter to a woman who had reached almost twenty-four years of age without experimenting and he had taken it from her. Carelessly, thoughtlessly, cruelly.

'I took advantage of you last night,' Luciano breathed in a driven undertone. 'I was angry. I was drunk.'

Her pale blue eyes widened and she set down her cup with a sharp little snap. 'No, nobody took advantage of anyone last night. I'm an adult and I made a choice.'

'You weren't in any fit state to make a choice.'

Anger flared in her mutinous gaze. 'I chose you because I've never been so attracted to anyone before. I'm not proud that I was that shallow but it *was* my decision!'

Silence lay thick and heavy between them in the

heat and she shifted uneasily in her seat, embarrassed by her own vehemence. Had she really had to admit that she had never wanted any man the way she had wanted him? Didn't that sound a bit pathetic?

'The odd thing about decisions is that when you make major ones you're always convinced that you'll never change your mind. After my wife died in the crash I decided that I would *never* marry again,' Luciano confessed tautly, unsettling her with that admission. 'I did not want to share my life with another woman but I was grieving for the child I had lost and I did still want to be a parent. That is why I came up with the idea of a surrogacy agreement. I thought it would be a simple business contract and problem free, but I didn't count on dealing with a woman like your sister.'

Jemima heaved a sigh but said nothing. By running away with Nicky after the birth, Julie had changed everyone's lives and there was no getting away from that. She was, however, far more interested in wondering why Luciano had decided never to remarry. Had that been a tribute to the wife he loved? Gigi Nocella had been a gorgeous and very famous movie star. What woman could possibly follow in such gilded footsteps?

'You have had complete responsibility for my son since he was only a few days old,' Luciano pointed out.

'Yes.' Jemima snapped back to the present and shook irritably free of her futile speculation about Luciano's past. 'Julie went back to London to work. She told me that she earned good money working in PR and I had no reason to doubt her. I continued my teaching job and placed Nicky in a nursery nearby. Julie didn't help with the expense and it was a challenge to afford it on my salary and my savings were soon gone. My parents were struggling too, so it made sense for me to give up my apartment and move home again.'

'You've made sacrifices to look after my son,' Luciano acknowledged grimly. 'And you have looked after him well. I believe that you love him and that he loves you.'

'I couldn't help loving him.' Jemima sighed.

'But he's not your child.'

Jemima grimaced at that unnecessary reminder. 'That didn't come into it for me.'

Luciano continued to study her with brooding intensity. 'My son may not be your child now but he *could* be...'

Jemima stared back at him in bewilderment. 'What on earth are you saying?' she framed uncertainly.

'I'm asking you to marry me to become my son's mother and my wife,' Luciano clarified with silken sibilance, his dark eyes glimmering golden as a lion's in the sunlight. 'It makes sense—in this situation it makes the very best sense. Think about it and you'll see that.'

CHAPTER EIGHT

JEMIMA WAS IN SHOCK.

Luciano Vitale was asking her to marry him. How was that possible? She had joined him at breakfast expecting to be told when she would be flying home and instead he had proposed marriage. Her lashes fluttered down to screen her eyes.

'Nicky's mother?'

'And the mother of any other children that we might have together,' Luciano slotted in smoothly, catching her startled upward glance and looking steadily back at her. 'I'm talking about a normal marriage and a family. Be assured of that.'

Jemima felt rather like a mouse cornered by a cat. His brilliant dark eyes sought out hers, level and direct and forceful, as if seeking assurance that she was listening properly. A normal marriage, a *family*. Shock was piling on shock. Her taut lips parted and she blurted out, 'But you're not in love with me!'

Luciano inclined his arrogant head to one side and compressed his sensual mouth. 'Is that kind of romantic love so necessary to you?'

Jemima went pink. 'I always assumed that I would only marry for love.'

'But love doesn't always last,' Luciano parried wryly. 'It can also encourage unrealistic expectations in the relationship. I can't offer you love but I can offer you respect and consideration and fidelity. I believe there is a very good chance that a marriage created on such practical foundations would succeed.'

She thought he was quite probably the most beautiful man in the world as he leant back against that balustrade, black curls ruffling in the breeze above his darkly handsome features. He was offering her respect, consideration and fidelity. Didn't he believe in love? Or did he still think he was in love with his first wife? She wanted to ask but it felt like the wrong moment. Luciano had proposed marriage. Wasn't that supposed to be special? It was obvious he had thought in depth about marrying her.

'Why me?' she asked baldly.

'Primarily you love my son and he loves you. I grew up without a mother and I want more for him.'

'You could marry anyone,' she cut in helplessly.

'But to any other woman Niccolò would always be second best once she had a child of her own. I don't believe you will react like that but many women would,' Luciano fielded quietly.

'Yet you planned his birth knowing you intended to raise your child without a mother,' she reminded him.

'That was before I saw the strength of the bond between you and him and the happiness that gave him.'

Having heard enough, Jemima forced a smile and

rose from her seat. 'I'm afraid the man I marry would have to want me for more than my child-rearing abilities,' she told him stiffly, struggling to keep the little amused smile in place and mask the deep hollow of hurt opening up inside her.

Luciano dealt her a seething look of frustration and strode after her. 'Jemima!'

Jemima didn't turn her head, she just kept on walking away fast, unable to face any further dialogue. She was so hurt and she didn't really understand why. Surely it was always a sort of a compliment if a man asked you to marry him? Even if you didn't want to say yes. And at that point, she realised what was wrong. She wanted *more*. She wanted him to want her personally and that was downright silly as well as unlikely. So many more beautiful and sophisticated women would have snatched at Luciano's offer with two greedy hands. Who did she think she was to be so finicky?

'Jemima…!' Luciano exclaimed, closing a powerful hand round her shoulder to spin her round in the picture gallery. 'You know very well that I want you for more than that!'

Jemima sucked in a gulp of oxygen and almost lost it again as she clashed with blazing dark golden eyes. 'Do I?' she slashed back in challenge.

'You *do* know,' Luciano told her, crowding her back against the wall behind her.

'How *would* I know?' Jemima flamed back at him. 'Nicky loves me and you think I'm good for him. That's why you're asking me to marry you.'

His white teeth flashed against his bronzed skin. 'Last night, we—'

'No, don't try to drag last night into it,' Jemima warned angrily. 'Your proposal made it clear that providing your son with a mother was your main motivation!'

'*Accidenti*... I was taking a conservative approach. I assumed you would prefer that!'

'Why would a woman want a conservative proposal?' Jemima countered impatiently.

'You would've preferred me to take you to bed again before I proposed?'

Jemima recognised the difference between her outlook and his and almost screamed in vexation. She thought of love and romance while he thought of sex, and wild, raunchy sex at that. Well, he had been upfront about not being able to offer love, so what more could she reasonably expect from him? And did she really *want* to say no? No to being Nicky's mum? No to being Luciano's wife and the potential mother of his children?

Luciano planted his hands squarely on the wall either side of her head, his lean, powerful body effectively imprisoning hers. Her ice-blue eyes widened as she felt his erection push against her belly, his hard readiness formidable even through the barrier of their clothes. Heat coiled at the heart of her rose up and clear thought process broke down. Hunger settled in a tight, hard knot inside her, constricting her breathing.

'No. On bended knee and dinner by candlelight would have been more your style,' Luciano derided.

'I'm not that old-fashioned,' she told him in exasperation.

Lowering his head, he brushed his lips almost teasingly against hers and then lingered to capture and suckle her lower lip, one hand sliding down the wall to close on her hip and jerk her into closer contact. His tongue eased between her readily parted lips and delved in an unashamedly sexual sortie. Her breathing fractured as she came off the wall to wrap her arms round his neck, fingertips sliding into his luxuriant hair.

'So, is this a yes, *piccolo mia*?' Luciano husked sexily against her swollen mouth.

'Are you *always* calculating the odds?' Jemima complained, jerking her head back out of reach.

Luciano gave her a wicked grin that loosed a flock of butterflies in her tummy and left her feeling dizzy. 'I don't switch off my brain very often,' he admitted.

She could have him if she wanted him, Jemima reflected on a heady high. And she wanted him—oh, my goodness, yes, she wanted him. But it would be crazy to make an impulsive decision based on the feelings of the moment. And her feelings just then were overwhelmingly physical and dangerously unreliable. Close to Luciano, her body vibrated like a tuning fork. He made her want to drag him off to the nearest secluded corner. That awareness cooled her heated blood and made her take a mental step back to take stock.

'I have to think about this,' Jemima declared, ignoring the frowning slant of his black brows above his stunning eyes. 'I need to be on my own for a while. I'm going for a walk on the beach.'

Recalling the flight of winding stone steps that led down to the shore from the terrace, she walked back into the sunlight. Round and round and round she went, moving faster and faster in her need to escape until her heels finally sank into the blissfully soft sand at the bottom. With a sigh she slipped off her shoes, closed her fingers through the straps and walked barefoot down to the shore.

The surf dampened her feet as she moved away from the castle. Little white houses straggled up the hillside on the other side of the horseshoe-shaped bay and boats bobbed in the harbour. A church with a bell tower made the village look even more picturesque in the sunshine.

So, how did she really feel about Luciano? Did she want him for the right reasons? Shouldn't Nicky be her driving motivation? Did it matter that she was thinking less about Nicky and more about becoming Luciano's wife? Why couldn't she think about anything but Luciano? Was she infatuated with him? No doubt that would wear off with continued exposure to him and prevent her from behaving like an embarrassing teenager with a crush, she thought with an inner wince. After all, it was obvious that if such a marriage of convenience was to work she would have to be more practical in her outlook.

Could she happily settle for respect and consideration and fidelity? Well, she thought wryly, maybe not *happily*, but, if the alternative was not to have Luciano at all, her choice was being made for her. If the chance was there, she definitely wanted to take it and give it a go. And what about her family, her friends and the teaching career that she loved? Living abroad in Sicily? Could she adjust to that change? Friends and family would be able to visit as she would be able to visit them, she told herself, and, while she would miss her job, raising Nicky and having more children would certainly fill her time.

Registering that she was walking straight for the natural rock formation that cut off the beach at one point, Jemima changed direction in favour of the path running between the shore and the single-track road. She put her shoes back on, relieved she had worn low heels, and only as she straightened did she appreciate that she was not walking alone. Three of Luciano's bodyguards hovered several yards away and she made a shooing motion of dismissal with her hands before turning defiantly on her heel and picking up her pace towards the village. Why on earth were they following her? Were such precautions really necessary for her safety?

Tired and hot, she paused at a café above the beach and walked in to sit down. It was busy. A large group of elderly men sat playing a board game in one corner and several other tables were occupied. As soon as Jemima sat down a bodyguard approached her to ask her what she wanted, acting as a liaison between her and the proprietor, who was viewing them nervously. Freshly squeezed orange juice was brought and she sipped, cooling off from the early-morning heat while watching a handful of children play ball on the beach below.

Nicky would have a whole beach to himself at the castle, she thought heavily. Would he even be allowed to play with other children? Had Luciano the smallest idea of what an ordinary childhood was like? What had his own been like? He had shared so little with her. All she knew about his background and his first marriage had been gleaned from the Internet. Luciano was not a male who willingly opened up about his past.

A sports car purred to a halt outside and Luciano sprang out of it. The proprietor bowed almost double and the waiter copied him. The old men stopped their game, suddenly rigid, their chatter silenced. As he strode in Luciano addressed the owner and then settled down lithely opposite her, seemingly impervious to the apprehensive silence that had greeted his arrival and that of his protection team.

'Why did you have me followed?'

'My father died when his yacht was blown up in the harbour out there,' Luciano volunteered. 'I have lived a very different life but there are still those who hate and fear me because of the blood in my veins. I can't take the risk of ignoring that.'

Jemima had gone very pale. She brushed his hand soothingly with her fingers. 'I'm sorry...'

His lush lashes lifted and dark golden eyes scanned her as a glass of water was brought to the table for him. 'For what? For old history? Nobody grieved for my father, least of all me,' he admitted bluntly.

'Was your childhood unhappy?' she murmured tautly, her eyes on his lean, dark face and the strong tension etched there.

'Is knowing such things about me important to you?'

Amazed that he should have to ask that, Jemima nodded confirmation.

Luciano drank his water. 'It was a nightmare,' he admitted gruffly. 'That's why I want a normal family life for Niccolò.'

Jemima wondered what a nightmare entailed and wasn't sure she could live with further clarification. The haunting darkness in his eyes sent a chill racing down her spine. The old men in the corner were still staring and she glanced away, wondering what it had been like for Luciano to grow up as the son of a man who was loathed and feared and whose reputation for corruption had stretched beyond death to shadow his son's. Frustrated tenderness laced with intense compassion twisted through Jemima. A normal family life. It was not so much to ask. It was not an impossible dream, was it? In fact it was a modest aspiration for so wealthy and powerful a male and that knowledge touched her heart more deeply than anything else could have done.

Luciano wondered why Jemima appeared to be on the brink of tears. He could see moisture glimmering in her ice-blue eyes. He didn't want to talk about his dirty past; he didn't even want to think about such things. It had soiled him for ever—how could it not soil her? Furthermore, he was still reeling from his own behaviour the night before: he had lost control of his temper and acted with dishonour. Even his father had waited to marry his mother before sharing a bed with her. He repressed his troubled thoughts, knowing the futility of regretting what was past.

'I want to marry you,' he told her very quietly.

'I know,' she whispered, her heart beating so fast it felt as though it were in her throat. 'But I'm not sure what that means to you.'

'I wanted you the first moment I saw you,' Luciano ground out in a driven undertone. 'Is that what you want to hear? I thought you were your sister then and I couldn't believe that I could want such a woman, so I fought it. You're a very loving woman, Jemima, and my son needs that. I don't think I'm capable of giving that kind of love, but you are.'

Yes, that was what Jemima had needed to hear. A blinding smile curved her lips and lit up her face. 'OK...you've won me over,' she told him shakily.

Luciano snapped his fingers and the proprietor came running. He spoke in Italian. The waiter scurried around serving everyone in the bar, even Luciano's protection team. The café owner reappeared with a dusty bottle, which he proffered with pride. The wine was poured and toasts were made.

'I bought everyone a drink to celebrate our wedding plans with us,' Luciano explained as her eyes widened.

'We're talking weddings now?' Jemima parroted as he nudged her nerveless fingers with a wine glass. 'You want me to have a drink? But it's only ten o'clock in the morning!'

He groaned out loud and raked impatient fingers through his black curls. '*Santa Madonna!* I forgot to give you the ring!'

In a daze, Jemima moistened her dry mouth with the wine. 'There's a ring?'

'*Certamente*…of course there's a ring!' Luciano withdrew a tiny box from his pocket and flipped it open to a spectacular sapphire ring surrounded by diamonds. Removing it from the box, he lifted her hand and slid it onto her engagement finger. 'If you don't like it, we can choose something else.'

'No…it's beautiful,' Jemima whispered dizzily. 'Where did you get it from? I mean, we only arrived…'

'It belonged to my mother's family…and no, before you ask, it never belonged to Gigi,' he assured her.

Smiles had broken out all around them. Several solemn toasts were made. Luciano seemed taken aback by the warmth of the good wishes offered. Jemima drank her wine and watched the sunlight glitter off her amazing ring while wondering with a little frisson of excitement if Luciano would be sharing a bed with her again that night.

'Why did Gigi never wear this ring?' she asked baldly.

'It wasn't flashy enough for her. She only wore diamonds.'

It was the first time he had voluntarily mentioned his first wife. Jemima supposed that in time she would learn more but she could tell by his tension that, although he was trying hard to be more open with her, it was a tender subject and he was struggling. So much had already changed between them but the biggest alteration in Luciano's attitude had occurred as soon as he'd realised that she wasn't her twin sister, Julie. The awareness that he had fought any attraction to her before he'd known her true identity soothed Jemima's concerns. Luciano was willing to overlook her lies because he respected her attachment to Nicky and her principles. In other words, what was important to her was equally important to him.

'So, when will we be getting married?' she asked as Luciano tucked her into the elegant sports car outside.

'As soon as possible. Draw up a guest list of friends and family.' Curling black lashes shaded Luciano's gaze, his wide sensual mouth relaxed. 'My staff will take care of all the arrangements. We'll have the wedding here.'

Her eyes widened. '*Here* in Sicily?'

'I don't think it would be a good idea to trail Niccolò back to the UK again,' Luciano commented with a frown. 'You would have to stay somewhere where my security people could look after you both because when word of our relationship breaks in the media you will both be a paparazzi target. It will be easier if you remain here on the island, where your privacy can be assured.'

Jemima tried to absorb the realities of her new life and slowly shook her head in bemusement because she could not even begin to imagine being a target for the paparazzi. But, more importantly, a further change of climate and yet another selection of strange faces would not benefit Nicky either, she conceded ruefully. If Castello del Drogo was to be the little boy's permanent home, he should be allowed to settle into his new surroundings without the stress of having to adapt to any additional challenges.

'I have a tour of Asia scheduled and, as I'll be away

for a couple of weeks, I suggest that you invite your family out to keep you company until the wedding,' Luciano remarked, disconcerting her.

He was leaving her. Jemima refused to betray any reaction. Obviously he would travel on business and such temporary separations would be part of their lives. She had never been the clingy type. She was independent and self-sufficient, she reminded herself doggedly. Wanting to climb into his suitcase with Nicky was just plain stupid.

'I'm surprised you're prepared to leave Nicky so soon,' she admitted.

'When the tour of my holdings was organised, actually finding my son still seemed like a fantasy,' he confided ruefully. 'Now that I have found him I have no intention of being an absent parent. Once I'm home again I'll be spending a lot of time with him.'

They returned to the *castello*. 'What made you buy this place?' Jemima asked curiously. 'Was it purely for the private setting?'

'I didn't buy it. I inherited it. It belonged to my mother's family. She grew up here.' His lean bronzed face shadowed.

'Did you stay here when you were a child?'

'No. My mother never returned after she married my father. He first saw her playing on the beach down there as a teenager,' Luciano told her, tight-mouthed. 'When I was older he called it love at first sight. I would call it lust...'

Like what Luciano had felt on first seeing Jemima? Jemima wondered ruefully. An instant attraction, similar to what she herself had felt, so how could she look down on that?

'How did they get together?' she prompted.

'In a decent world they would never have got together. He was a murderer, a thief, a gangster,' Luciano declared without any expression. 'She was the adored only child of a titled, educated man. But that man gambled and got into debt and my father bought his debt and soon my father owned him. My father wrote off the debt in return for my mother's hand in marriage…'

'My goodness,' Jemima said sickly. 'What did she have to say about it?'

'She loved her father and she did what she had to do to save him from the shame of bankruptcy,' Luciano revealed. 'I can't imagine she was happy about the price she had to pay. She married a brutal man.'

Jemima heard the chill in his dark-timbred voice and decided it was definitely time to change the subject. He didn't want to talk about his parents' marriage and in the circumstances that was hardly surprising. As she recalled, his mother had died when he was only three years old and it was unlikely that he remembered much about the beautiful brunette in the portrait on the stairs. It was something they had in common and she commented on the fact.

Luciano turned frowning eyes on her.

'Have you forgotten that I was adopted? I don't remember anything about my birth parents but what I do know now, thanks to Julie's research, is that there's nothing there to be proud of. Our birth mum was a drug addict and I'll never know who our father was.'

The grim edge stamped round his beautiful mouth eased. 'Ignorance could be bliss.'

'Leave it in the past where it belongs,' she urged, closing her hand round his. 'We're not responsible for what our parents did, nor do we have to resemble them.'

Luciano smiled at her simplistic advice and her un-subtle attempt to offer him comfort. He didn't need comfort. He knew who he was and where he had come from and what he had to avoid to achieve a reasonably happy and successful life. Caring too much about any-thing, be that women, work or money, was what he had surrendered to embrace peace of mind.

Nicky was surfacing from a nap when they entered the nursery and he held out his arms to Jemima with a huge smile. She hauled him up and turned to Luci-ano with a grin, wanting to include him, wanting to encourage father and son to get to know each other properly. 'Let's take him down to the beach. He's never seen the sea.'

She changed into her serviceable and rather faded blue racer-back swimsuit, unable to face the challenge of modelling one of the daring 'barely there' bikini sets in her new wardrobe. Luciano joined her in swim shorts, lifting a delighted Nicky high and smiling with satisfaction when the little boy laughed. She watched the long, lithe line of his muscled back flex as he tucked Nicky securely below one arm and strode downstairs. Not an ounce of fat clung to his well-built physique and it showed in his narrow waist and lean hips.

A picnic lunch was delivered and food for Nicky. The baby loved getting his toes wet in the surf. He loved even more being held up in the air and looking down at his father. Jemima watched father and son, relieved at how naturally they could interact in a more relaxed setting. Clearly no longer uneasy in Luciano's presence, Nicky dug his hands into his father's hair and touched his face with growing familiarity.

'That was a good suggestion,' Luciano told her appreciatively as they headed back to the *castello*.

A blonde waved and smiled at them from the terrace as they climbed the steps up from the beach. She surged forward to greet Luciano and kiss him Continental-style on both cheeks. She was a beauty, a tall, slender blonde with dark eyes and great dress sense.

'Jemima, meet Sancia Abate…' Luciano made the introduction casually. 'Sancia, my wife-to-be, Jemima, and my son, Niccolò.'

Sancia barely glanced in Jemima's direction but fussed in a very feminine way over Nicky.

'Who is she? Does she work for you?' Jemima asked as they walked away.

'No. She's Gigi's kid sister,' he confided, startling her. 'I still let her use the guest house here when she needs a break. Nicky gets tired quickly, doesn't he?'

Jemima watched the baby stick his thumb in his mouth and close his eyes against her shoulder and she smiled in spite of her surprise at that revelation concerning the svelte blonde. 'You exhausted him. He's not used to that kind of play. My father's past that stage.'

'But he's very fond of him,' Luciano cut in.

'Yes, he is. Did you have grandparents?'

'No, my grandfather died soon after my parents

married.' His strong jaw clenched, his mouth flattening. 'Agnese was my nurse when I was a child. She was the closest thing I had to a grandparent.'

'I didn't have any either. Mum and Dad met and married later in life,' Jemima told him as she passed Nicky over to Carlotta in the hall and joined Luciano on the stairs. 'You lost your mother young.'

'Yes.'

'How did it happen?'

Luciano strode across the landing without answering her.

'Was she ill?' Jemima persisted, following him down the stone passageway and into his room.

'No,' Luciano gritted impatiently, slamming the door closed behind him with a frustrated hand. 'Don't you take hints? I don't want to talk about this...'

Jemima reddened uncomfortably, feeling like a rude nosy parker for having continued to ask questions even after he walked away. 'I'm sorry...'

His lustrous dark golden eyes glittered. 'No, I don't want to lie but I don't want to tell you the truth either.'

She turned round and smoothed her hands up over his cheekbones in what was meant to be a comforting and apologetic gesture. 'I'm a horribly nosy person,' she confessed guiltily. 'Give me an inch and I'll take a mile. Don't even *hint* at a secret...it turns me into a bloodhound that won't quit!'

Reluctant laughter escaped Luciano. He stared down at her anxious face and a deep hunger for the warmth of her engulfed him in a tidal wave of need. He pulled her into his arms and claimed her mouth with devastating urgency.

Taken by surprise, Jemima laughed and then gasped beneath the savage onslaught of his mouth. Her body caught flame like hay, a burning ache stirring between her legs, a hot, prickling awareness stiffening her nipples.

'*Madonna!* I think I'll die if I don't have you now,' Luciano growled, long fingers closing into the shoulders of her swimsuit to wrench it down and release her breasts.

He tumbled her down on his bed and skimmed off his shorts in an impatient motion, coming up on the mattress to join her unashamedly naked and eager. He knelt at her feet and yanked her swimsuit down her hips to toss it aside while his smouldering gaze wandered at will over her splayed body.

'I love these…so pretty, so lush,' he husked, his fingers cupping the curves of her high, full breasts before rising to stroke the pouting crests. 'And these.' A lean hand travelled up a slender thigh and nudged her legs apart to display a tantalising ribbon of soft, glistening pink. 'And *this* perfect place, *piccolo mia.* I am enslaved…'

He found that feminine perfection with the erotic expertise of his mouth and it was magical and then terrifying to lose control so fast. She clutched at his hair. She sobbed. She gasped. Ultimately she cried his name in an ecstasy of quivering, wanton pleasure, her body weak and heavy with satisfaction as she lay beneath him, too stunned by his passion and the explosive response he had roused from her to move again.

'What was it about me…er…being nosy that set you off?' she whispered helplessly.

Luciano's brow furrowed. He honestly didn't know. He had looked at her and an uncontrollable urge to take her to bed had overpowered him. He couldn't explain it. Her wild response to him had soothed the savage turmoil inside him in a manner beyond his comprehension. He touched her with gentle fingers, put his mouth to a rose-pink nipple, toying with her for a few moments, smiling against her flushed skin as she muttered his name as though she were saying a prayer. He turned her over onto her stomach. She complained about being moved and he ignored it, lifting her up, aligning their bodies and then plunging into the damp, silken heat of her with a raw groan of enthusiasm, swiftly echoed by her boneless cry of encouragement.

Delicious sensation ricocheted up through Jemima's body, building from the hot, aching heart of her into a blaze that consumed as Luciano slammed into her with compelling strength. Her excitement climbed with the sweet, earthy delight of his penetration. And just when she believed that powerful excitement couldn't reach any greater height he sent her flying into an orgasm that snapped taut her every muscle and blew her apart in a sublime surge of drowning, melting pleasure.

'Oh…wow…' Jemima mumbled, flopping down against the pillows.

Luciano flipped her over and gathered her damp, trembling body close. 'Oh…wow…' he teased. 'Well, you have no choice but to marry me now.'

'How's that?' she framed, barely able to think straight.

'I didn't use a condom—'

Her brows pleated in dismay. 'Luciano—'

'Having unprotected sex is a sign of commitment, which I have never risked before with a woman,' he announced above her head.

'You want a brass trophy or something?' Jemima looked up at him with wry amusement.

'No, I want a repeat…' Luciano growled, treating her full lower lip to a tiny carnal nip swiftly followed by a soothing stroke of his tongue. 'That was the best sex I ever had, *piccolo mia.*'

'Good, because you won't have got me pregnant,' Jemima told him with assurance. 'It's the wrong time of the month for that.'

Luciano stared down at her with brooding intensity, his lean, darkly handsome features set in unsettlingly serious lines. 'Don't be too curious with me.'

Jemima had become very still and her eyes were troubled. 'Why not?'

'Unlike you, I'm not the sharing type. I have too much stuff to hide.'

'Red rag to a bull, Luciano,' Jemima warned. 'And if we're getting married there's nothing you should need to hide from me.'

Luciano sat up, his dark eyes veiled, his lean, strong body taut with tension. 'My father killed my mother when I was three,' he breathed in a constrained undertone. 'She was trying to take me and leave him… He threw her down the stairs and she broke her neck. I saw it happen.'

Jemima froze and then consciously unfroze again to

close her arms protectively round him. 'How horrible for you to be forced to live with a memory like that.'

Luciano was rigid in the circle of her arms. 'It's my past.'

'Yes...*past*,' Jemima stressed, stringing a line of haphazard kisses along the clenched line of his strong jaw until some of his tension eased.

He frowned down at her. 'Doesn't it bother you, knowing what I just told you?'

'Not as much as it bothered you telling me.'

'I've never told anyone before,' he breathed into her hair. 'I used to have nightmares about it.'

'And who comforted you then?' she whispered.

'Agnese...she was always there for me. She saw it happen too.'

'And nobody went to the police?'

'My father had too many friends in high places and corrupt connections within the police. My mother's death was written off as a tragic accident and he got away with it. By the time I was old enough to do any different he was dead. But he would have killed anyone who stood as a witness against him, even if I had been the witness,' he explained heavily. 'That was his life. That is the kind of environment that I grew up with and it is exactly those experiences that made me swear that I would never ever be like my father in any way.'

'And you've lived up to that promise,' Jemima re-minded him quietly. 'Haven't you?'

'Yes, *piccolo mia.*'

'So, you should be proud of what you have achieved and celebrating your success,' Jemima told him, shifting her hips in the hope of giving his thoughts a different direction.

Being highly suggestible, Luciano lifted his tousled head with a sudden smile and kissed her again with all the pent-up fire of his hot temperament. She smiled up at him, satisfied that she had finally got behind his barriers, broken through the hard shell to the real man within. He didn't have to love her to confide in her. Somehow at that instant it seemed more than sufficient compensation.

CHAPTER NINE

'COME FOR TEA, said the spider to the fly,' Ellie mocked with a grimace. 'I don't like Sancia.'

Jemima wrinkled her nose. Her best friend, Ellie, was very quick in her judgements but Jemima tried to give everyone a fair hearing. And that included Sancia Abate, the gorgeous blonde who had stepped unannounced and unforeseen out of Luciano's past. After all, Jemima would have been the first to admit that the main source of her unease about Sancia was the other woman's close blood tie to Luciano's celebrated first wife. Luciano, however, had been so casual about the continuing friendship that only an extremely jealous and possessive woman could have been suspicious of the relationship. Sancia was evidently still accepted as family and Jemima was happy to respect that.

In any case, she had to admit that Sancia had proved to be an almost invisible guest over the past two weeks while Luciano had been abroad. For the past three days, Jemima had been entertaining Ellie and her parents' friends and relatives, all of whom Luciano had had flown out for the wedding that was scheduled to take place in forty-eight hours' time. Her parents and their closest friends had already settled into a comfortable routine of strolls on the beach and visits to the village café, while Jemima had whiled away many a happy hour trying on wedding dresses and relaxing with Ellie.

'I mean, what's a blonde that looks like that doing hanging round here on a very quiet island without even a boyfriend in tow?' Ellie remarked suspiciously.

Jemima had learned that Sancia was not only gorgeous to look at but also multitalented. Sancia had written a bestselling biography on her much-loved sister's life and currently seemed to drift between stints as a well-known fashion model and a less-well-known actress. The guest house was situated beyond the castle gardens above the beach, a former boathouse that had been renovated to offer extra accommodation. Bearing in mind the sheer size of the castle, the cottage was virtually never used.

Jemima was wryly amused that she had found it necessary to dress up to visit Sancia. More and more she was making use of the wardrobe Luciano had bought for her, recognising that the garments might be more fashionable and form-fitting than she was accustomed to wearing but were also more flattering in style and shape. To enjoy tea with the glamorous Sancia, she was wearing a lilac skirt and top with an unmistakeable designer edge.

'Oh, you haven't brought Nicky.' Sancia sighed in disappointment as soon as she opened the door. 'Come in.'

'He always has a nap straight after lunch.'

'*Porca miseria!* You sound like one of those rigid English nannies people joke about!' the blonde commented with a teasing smile.

'I hope not…' Jemima stilled on the threshold of a spacious reception room that was dominated by photos and portraits of Gigi Nocella.

'Oh, didn't you know that the guest house is where Luciano keeps his stash of memorabilia?' Sancia remarked in apparent surprise. 'I thought you would have guessed. I mean, there's nothing at all to be seen up at the castle.'

'No, nothing,' Jemima agreed, having naturally noticed that, surprisingly, Luciano had not a single photograph on display anywhere of his late first wife or their little daughter.

'I know. He had the place stripped…the poor guy.' Sancia sighed. 'Once Gigi was gone, he just couldn't live with even the *smallest* reminder of her. It was too painful for him. Haven't you noticed that he never ever mentions her?'

Jemima was not very practised at female games of one-upmanship but she knew enough to know when she was being targeted and she murmured quietly, 'Are we having tea?'

'I'm not very domesticated but I do have the tray ready for us.' Sancia gave her a wide grin, unperturbed by Jemima's cool intonation, and stepped out into the room that Jemima assumed held a kitchen.

Jemima hovered by the window overlooking the fabulous view of the beach before succumbing to a curiosity that she simply couldn't suppress. The room she stood in was ironically both her worst nightmare and her most precious discovery. All around her sat the means to satisfy her curiosity about Luciano's first wife. Giving way to temptation, Jemima wandered around peering at the photos and the paintings.

There was no denying that Gigi Nocella had been superbly photogenic and immensely gifted in the genes department. The brown-eyed blonde, of whom Sancia was but a pale, more youthful copy, was exquisite to a degree very few women were and had reputedly been mesmerising on-screen. And here she was represented in all her earthly glory in various attitudes that ran from young and naïve to sexy and smouldering to pensive and mysterious. But the photos that Jemima paid most heed to were the ones that also contained Luciano.

The first she noted was their wedding photograph, in which he looked ridiculously youthful, reminding her that he had been very young when he married and that Gigi had been several years older.

'He worshipped the ground she walked on,' Sancia murmured from behind Jemima, making her flinch.

'Oh, my goodness, you gave me a fright!' Jemima spun and fanned the air, refusing to react to the blonde's provocative statement.

In any case, she didn't need the verbal commentary when she could see the adoration etched in Luciano's lean dark face as he looked intently at the mother of his daughter. It hurt Jemima to see that light in his eyes. She knew that he would never look at her with that depth of caring and concern. She would never be that important to him or that perfect in looks and figure that every head would turn to watch her walk by. No, she conceded sadly, she was in a totally different category from Gigi and, whether she liked it or not, Luciano would probably not have looked twice at her had his son not looked at Jemima with love first.

But she would have to learn to live with that reality, wouldn't she?

'After the crash, Luciano said he would never ever love a woman again,' Sancia delivered.

'Ah, well, life moves on and now he's getting married and he's starting another family,' Jemima responded with deliberate insensitivity before adding, 'It's different for you, though, as her sister. You'll never be able to replace her and you must miss her terribly.'

Red coins of colour accentuated the blonde's cheekbones. 'You have no idea.'

'I do actually. I didn't know my sister for very long before I lost her but there was a special bond there... at least on my side,' Jemima confided.

With hindsight she had begun to accept that her twin had not had the capacity to care for others in the same way as she did. She could not argue with the evidence and it was surely better for her to remember her sibling as she had been rather than idealise her memory.

'Gigi was irreplaceable,' Sancia told her a tad sharply.

'But I'm not trying to replace her,' Jemima responded quietly. 'How could I? And why would I even want to? Luciano and I have a completely different relationship.'

As Jemima walked back from the beach through

the castle gardens her pale blue eyes were overbright with tears. She didn't want to let the tears fall, not with her usual bodyguards bare yards from her, silent and watchful of her every move. Furthermore she had not the slightest doubt that anything unusual she did would be reported straight back to Luciano, who seemed to worry a great deal about her while he was away from her. He phoned her several times a day and questioned her right down to asking what she ate at mealtimes. And when she had asked him why he bothered when she had so little news to relate, he had told her teasingly that he liked the sound of her voice and could listen to her reciting an old phone book just as happily. The minutiae of Nicky's day were of equal interest to him and it was obvious to Jemima that Luciano really did miss seeing his son. His conversations with her, however, were just polite and sort of flirty, she reasoned ruefully. He wasn't a teenager, after all, he was a man of almost thirty-one with sufficient experience to know exactly how to charm a woman.

Especially if that woman wasn't Gigi Nocella, Jemima thought, her throat closing over convulsively on a sob. He wouldn't have had to make a special effort to say the right thing to a woman as perfect as Gigi had been. So, how often did he go down to visit that personal shrine in the guest house? If Jemima hadn't existed and Luciano hadn't been away on business, would he have been with Sancia right now happily reminiscing about the old days when his first wife and child had still been alive? It was hardly any wonder that Sancia resented Jemima and clearly felt threatened by her appearance on scene. Nothing could put Gigi more effectively back into the past than her once-besotted widower having another child and taking a second wife to put in Gigi's place.

Well, it wasn't Gigi's place any longer, Jemima told herself urgently. In less than two days Jemima would be Luciano's wife and she could hardly wait! She wasn't so silly as to allow Sancia's mean outlook to affect her personally, was she?

As her mobile phone rang she dug it out, grateful for an interruption that would hopefully give her thoughts a new and more positive direction. When she heard Steven's familiar badgering tones she almost groaned, however, for she had thought she had heard the last from her ex-boyfriend when he had phoned her to say he wouldn't be attending the wedding—he hadn't been invited!—because he knew she was making a dreadful mistake.

'Luciano has turned your head with his wealth,' Steven told her, merely starting a new angle of attack.

'His wealth doesn't matter to me. His kindness does,' Jemima parried, thinking of the generosity of Luciano's invitation to her parents and their friends, who were all enjoying a wonderful holiday in the run-up to their wedding. And by bringing her family and Ellie out to join her, he had ensured that she wasn't lonely and without support.

'You may not see it but I see very clearly that you are paying me back for what happened with Julie.' Steven sighed. 'You weren't able to forgive me.'

'I *did* forgive you, Steven. I simply didn't want to

take back up again where we'd left off and I think that's fair enough,' Jemima fielded. 'I saw you in a different light when you were with my sister.'

'I made a dreadful mistake, Jemima,' Steven groaned. 'But I *do* love you.'

'Not the way you loved her,' Jemima told him without heat.

'That wasn't genuine love and you don't love Luciano either. You're marrying him to keep Nicky,' Steven protested.

Jemima sat down on a stone bench surrounded by glorious rose beds and stared out blindly at the magnificent view of the bay. 'That's not true.'

'Marriage is a sacrament and it shouldn't be used.'

'But I *do* love him,' Jemima heard herself say and her whole mental view of the world lurched as she made that belated discovery. She was thinking about the male who had chilled her at first meeting and travelling at supersonic speed through the whole history of their relationship, ranging from his laughter in bed with her to the brutal background that he had triumphed over.

And there at the very heart of all her turmoil was the love she had neither acknowledged nor understood. She loved Luciano with all her being and easily zeroed in on every kind and caring thing he did for her from his hesitant tendering of his mother's ring for their engagement to his patient, undemanding love for Nicky in which he was willing to wait and earn his son's trust and affection. In the same moment she recognised why her encounter with Sancia and Gigi's shrine in the guest house had distressed her so much. It had hurt to see Luciano's love for her predecessor. It had hurt even more to frankly admit that she could never emulate such a woman to win that level of appreciation. With Luciano, she would always be Nicky's loving stepmother first and his wife second. Second best, second best for all time...

Could she truly live with that?

'Sorry, Steven. I have to go,' she said, cutting the call on Steven's expostulations with relief.

Her face was wet with tears. She had been crying without knowing it and she mopped her face, praying her mascara hadn't run. There could be no pleasure in appreciating that she would always be inferior in her future husband's eyes and heart to his first wife, but she was a practical, realistic woman and there really wasn't much she could do about that hurt. Was there?

She wouldn't even consider abandoning Nicky, for he felt as much her child as if he had been born to her rather than her sister. She saw no advantage to refusing to marry Luciano either. What would that achieve? She didn't want to be Nicky's nanny for the rest of her days or merely Luciano's lover. And if she didn't choose to marry him and give him more children, some other woman eventually would.

Not on my watch, Jemima conceded fiercely.

CHAPTER TEN

Something very like panic sent chilling tentacles travelling deep to pierce Luciano's usually rock-solid sense of security. He completed the phone call to his future relative, which had been preceded by one from Agnese. He had made a mistake, a *serious* mistake, he acknowledged with a sinking heart, and now he had to pray that he had sufficient time and the opportunity to put it right. And if he didn't?

Santa Madonna, that option could not even be considered!

Why the hell had he valued his pride above every other thing in his life for so many years? How on earth had he allowed a past bad experience to cast such a dangerous shadow over the present and potentially destroy his future?

And you thought you were so cool, so clever, he reasoned in a daze of growing shock at the mess he had created. But the creed of silence as a form of protection had been bred into his very bones at his father's knee. Never tell, never explain, never apologise. And before he had experienced that one weak moment with

Jemima he had *never* broken that rule. He had kept his secrets. He had kept them from the media too. Indeed he had buried those sleazy secrets deep and had refused even to think about them, for that was the safest, wisest way to hold on to sanity.

He had never dwelt on his mistakes because he was a rational man and it came naturally to him to move on past and not look back at car wrecks. Even so, those mistakes had seriously influenced the choices he had made, he conceded belatedly. Furthermore, Jemima didn't have his conditioning or his inhibitions and she would not understand...

The helicopter came in over the bay while Jemima was having breakfast with everyone in the shaded loggia on the ground floor. Nicky dropped his toast as he waved his hands with excitement, straining in his high chair to get a better view of the craft as it dropped down out of sight to land in the castle grounds.

'Is that Luciano coming back?' Ellie asked uncertainly.

'I doubt it. He's not due until tomorrow,' Jemima said a little tiredly because she had not slept well. 'And he's a stickler for his schedules.'

'I suspect,' her father murmured warmly as he stared over her shoulder, 'that your bridegroom missed you more than you know because here he is now...'

Jemima twisted her head round so fast she risked a whiplash injury and she thrust her chair back and stood up to stare in surprise at the male striding through the gardens towards them. It was, without a doubt, Luciano.

Sheathed in a dark business suit teamed with a white shirt and silvery tie, he looked both formal and formidable. His lean, darkly handsome face was taut, the line of his beautiful mouth forbidding. A jolt of dismay ran through Jemima and quite instinctively she found herself wondering if she had done something wrong.

His stunning dark golden eyes immediately sought hers as though he was looking for something and then he quickly turned his attention on to their guests and his first physical meeting with her parents. To a backdrop of Nicky's squeals of excitement and loud vocal appeals to be noticed, Luciano responded smoothly and pleasantly to the tide of introductions before stooping to detach Nicky from his harness and lift him into his arms.

'Hush,' he said softly to his son while ruffling his hair. 'You can't always be the centre of attention.'

'Well, when he isn't he likes to let us know he doesn't like it!' her father quipped cheerfully. 'He's a terrific little scene stealer.'

'Let me take him,' Jemima's mother urged, holding out her arms. 'You and Jemima should have some time together in peace.'

Nicky complained loudly at the transfer, demanded Jemima with pleading arms and then sobbed. Carlotta came out of the house to help while Jemima hovered, her attention anxiously pinned to Luciano, for all her nervous antennae were still telling her that something was badly wrong. His long, lean, powerful body was incredibly tense, his movements less fluid than usual and his lean, strong face taut with self-discipline.

Oh, my goodness, she thought in sudden consternation. Maybe he had returned early because he had changed his mind about marrying her! It was a nightmare scenario with the wedding guests and her family already staying at the castle, but it was perfectly possible that he had got cold feet and come back early to tell her. Jemima was quite convinced that such disasters had occurred to better women than her and it was surely more likely to happen when a man wasn't in love with the woman he had asked to marry him.

Luciano shot another veiled glance at Jemima. She was pale and there were shadows below her beautiful pale eyes and he could see that she looked nothing like a happy bride on the brink of her wedding. Inwardly he cursed himself again and he reached for her hand.

'Will you come for a walk with me?' he intoned in a roughened undertone. 'We have a visit to make.'

Her brow furrowed as he deftly walked her away from the breakfast table. 'A visit?'

'I believe you had tea with Sancia yesterday—'

'My goodness, the grapevine around here is positively supersonic!' Jemima countered while she thought fast.

'I like to keep an eye on events when I'm unable to be present in person,' Luciano assured her with a perfectly straight face.

Controlling...*much*? But Jemima said nothing because she knew that he was upset and she couldn't bear that. Glancing up at him, she could see the haunted look she had seen before was back in his eyes and she could see that, for all that he looked spectacular, he must have been travelling all night and lines of strain were etched between his classic nose and even more perfect mouth. Of course, if he wanted to cancel the wedding, he would be feeling awfully guilty about it, she thought painfully.

'What did you think of Sancia?'

'We don't have much in common,' Jemima replied mildly.

'She was a bitch to you, wasn't she?' Luciano growled within sight of the guest cottage above the beach.

Taken aback, Jemima came to a halt and stared up at him. 'I—'

'I can be selfish but I'm not stupid…most of the time,' Luciano tacked on, compressing his hard mouth. 'I've been foolish—'

'It's all right…whatever you decide to do, it's all right. Just don't be upset about it,' Jemima mumbled helplessly, resisting the urge to wrap both arms around him and offer him comfort. Even in the overly emotional mood she was in, she knew that was not the normal way to behave when a man dumped you and that the very last thing she should be worrying about was how *he* felt. And yet that urge was engrained in her when he was around, she thought painfully as he closed his hand firmly round hers and urged her on towards the cottage.

'Why are we going to see Sancia?' she prompted uncomprehendingly. 'I admit she wasn't the kindest hostess but I have nothing more to say to her.'

'But I have plenty to say,' Luciano incised, banging on the door with his fist.

Sancia opened the door little more than three seconds later. It was barely nine in the morning but she was wearing a pristine white sundress and had a full face of make-up on, so she had evidently been expecting visitors. 'Luciano…' she said, wreathed with welcoming smiles.

'Sancia…' he grated, moving past her to stare in shock at the array of photographs and paintings decorating the cottage living room. 'What is all this?' he breathed.

'Well, you should know,' the blonde said archly. 'You insisted on giving it to me.'

'You asked me for it—you wanted it for your book,' Luciano reminded her.

Only moments into their visit and Jemima was already feeling better, for she could already see that Luciano had had no part in creating the shrine in the room to his late wife. That, it seemed, had been solely Sancia's doing.

'It's been like this ever since the year she died,' the blonde fielded, playing it for all she was worth.

'You're the only person who has ever used this place.' Luciano released Jemima's hand and swept up a book from the coffee table. 'Wasn't the book enough for you?'

'I don't know what you mean?'

'Sancia, I was married to Gigi for five years. This isn't a biography, it's a work of fiction. You gave her fans what they wanted to read, not the truth. The truth would have been too ugly,' he breathed, his deep, dark drawl roughening along the edges.

Sancia switched to Italian and spoke at length.

'No, we will discuss this in English so that Jemima understands,' Luciano decreed grimly. 'I want to know what Sancia told you yesterday.'

'Nothing that was untrue,' Sancia trilled, sweetly saccharine. 'That you don't like to talk about Gigi and that you *said* you'd never love a woman again.'

Luciano grimaced. 'Sancia! Where is your compassion? Your sister almost destroyed me!'

'There is no need for you to tell—' Sancia began urgently.

'A couple who are about to marry should have no secrets from each other,' Luciano declared, and as Jemima stiffened in surprise he smiled ruefully. 'A very wise woman once told me that but I wasn't listening.'

'But you have never wanted the truth to come out!' Sancia was still arguing. 'You were happy for me to write a whitewash!'

'I've matured.' Luciano tossed the book back down on the table and looked at Jemima. 'Gigi was not the glowing star and wonderful woman described in this book. I married her because she told me I was the father of the child she carried. She was repeatedly unfaithful to me with the leading men in her movies, and the day she died she was leaving me for another man.'

'Oh, no...' Jemima mumbled, pained by the look in his eyes.

'That man, Alessio di Campo, is a famous producer and he was the love of Gigi's life—well, as much as she could love anyone, she loved him,' Luciano revealed doggedly. 'He was a married man with a wife and only when his wife died were the two of them willing to go public about their relationship. Their affair had, however, apparently continued throughout our marriage. I told her that she was welcome to leave but that I would not let her take our daughter, Melita, with her.'

'How can you trust her? She could go to the press with all this!' Sancia screeched accusingly.

'Jemima won't and even if the story was to get out, so what?' Luciano shrugged a broad shoulder with fluid fatalism. 'It's all done and dusted now. To finish the story, Gigi told me that Melita was *not* my daughter but Alessio's,' he revealed heavily. 'I had stayed in a bad marriage for years for my daughter's sake and suddenly she wasn't my child any more. That truth was more devastating than Gigi's departure with Melita that day.'

'It was a cruel lie,' Sancia swore, desperate to be heard again. 'I never believed that!'

'Testing was carried out after the crash,' Luciano cut in flatly, his lean, masculine face unrelentingly grim. 'Melita was *not* my child but I loved her as though she was and had she survived I would have kept her with me had I had the choice. As it was, both mother and child died instantly when the helicopter Alessio had sent to pick them up crashed on the flight to Monaco.'

Jemima's eyes were stinging. Only Sancia's sullen, resentful presence prevented her from saying what she really felt because her heart was bleeding for him. He had been hiding the truth from her all along and she was deeply shaken by the true version of what his marriage had entailed. It had not occurred to her that Gigi could have been anything less than perfect. In reality, though, Gigi had been a horribly disloyal and dishonest partner and Jemima was no longer surprised that Luciano had required DNA testing before he had been prepared to accept Nicky as his son.

'Let's go...' Luciano breathed, curving a protective arm to Jemima's spine.

'I could sell Gigi's *true* story for a fortune,' Sancia remarked quietly.

'Go ahead. I no longer care,' Luciano responded almost cheerfully. 'But if you go naming names you will probably make a lot of dangerous enemies amongst the very people whom you still want to employ you. But that's your business now that I will no longer be settling your bills. My pilot's waiting for you at the helipad. I'm sure I don't need to add that you're no longer welcome here.'

And with that final withering speech they were both back out in the fresh air and sunshine again. Shellshocked, Jemima leant against Luciano for a few seconds, revelling in the strength of his tall, powerful body and the gloriously familiar scent of him. All she could think about was that Gigi had been a dreadful liar and then Julie had lied to him and cheated him and then Jemima had lied to him as well! How could he ever fully forgive her for having lied to him after what he had had to endure in his first, unhappy marriage?

'You know... I thought you'd got cold feet about the wedding,' she told him dizzily. 'I believed you were back early to dump me—'

'No, I was too scared I was losing you. I didn't know

what Sancia had done but I always suspected she could be poisonous.'

'But how could you even find out that I was seeing her yesterday? The bodyguards?'

'No, Agnese. She's like a bloodhound. She phoned me to tell me that Sancia had invited you and informed me that that was suspicious because Sancia is not friendly towards other women.'

'Why were you paying Sancia's bills?'

'At first I felt sorry for her because she was always overshadowed by Gigi. Of course, she knew all her sister's dark secrets because she worked as Gigi's assistant on the Palermo estate we lived on in those days.' He hesitated. 'With the timing involved, nobody guessed that Gigi had been in the act of leaving me when she died and I told myself that it was my private business. But, more honestly, I chose to save face rather than tell the truth. The paparazzi had dogged us obsessively throughout our marriage because, of course, there were always rumours about Gigi's behaviour but she was never caught out.'

'I can understand you not wanting people to know that she had affairs,' Jemima murmured ruefully. 'It hurt your pride and Sancia played along with that because it suited her to do so.'

'She made a killing on the book because she wrote what Gigi's fans wanted to read. They didn't want to hear about the man-eater with the monstrous ego who seduced me when I was twenty-two and too rich and naïve to smell a rat. Of course, she was already pregnant when she first slept with me.'

'And you didn't even suspect?'

'I was infatuated with her. It was probably a little like the way you reacted to your unknown twin when she first turned up. I only saw what I wanted to see in Gigi and I was flattered by her interest.'

'But the marriage only lasted because of Melita?'

Luciano could not hide his sadness. 'The marriage died within months of Melita's birth. I loved that little girl and she loved me. Gigi had no interest in her daughter but she wouldn't have given up custody of her because she said that would damage her reputation as a mother.'

'And *did* you say that you would never love a woman again after her?'

'Yes,' Luciano admitted freely. 'Because loving Gigi was a horrendous experience and I couldn't forgive myself for being such a fool. I sincerely believed that it would only be safe to love a child, which is why I planned the surrogacy arrangement.'

'You do think in some seriously screwy ways sometimes,' Jemima told him gently.

His nostrils flared as he thrust open a side door into the castle. 'It seemed perfectly logical to me at the time. Gigi did a lot of damage and I didn't want to be burned again.'

'It was still a little over the top,' Jemima criticised. 'You may have decided to live without love but most children want two parents.'

Luciano shot her an impatient look. 'All right, I'm selfish...and maybe I didn't think it all through the way

I should have done. But look how it turned out,' he said with a sudden grin. 'I got you… Have I still got you?'

'It would take more than Sancia to scare me off.'

'Yet you actually thought I could be about to dump you?' An ebony brow quirked in wonderment. 'What makes you so modest? I cut my trip short a day and travelled all night to get to you because I heard that you were upset.'

Jemima stiffened. 'Who *said* I was upset?'

'I promised not to name names,' Luciano revealed.

'I wasn't upset yesterday,' Jemima insisted out of pride. 'I was just working through some stuff and thinking a lot. Getting married is a big challenge.'

'Especially when the groom is someone like me,' Luciano slotted in without hesitation. 'Someone too proud and private to admit that his first marriage was a disaster and that his first child wasn't his child.'

Jemima wrinkled her nose as he walked her up the rear staircase she had never used before. 'But I sort of understand you keeping quiet about that, although that doesn't mean I approve of you being that secretive.'

'And the prospect of marriage must become even more challenging for a woman when the bridegroom refuses to admit that he loves you,' Luciano told her in a rush shorn of the smallest eloquence. 'That wasn't just secretive, that was stupid, because if you'd known how much I love you yesterday you would have laughed in Sancia's face and I wouldn't have been panicked into rushing halfway across the world to assure myself that you weren't going to desert me.'

'I wouldn't desert you…or Nicky,' Jemima added,

still working very slowly through what he had said. 'You love me?'

'Insanely.' A flood of dark colour accentuated his high cheekbones. 'The thought of life without you downright terrifies me. A couple of weeks being without you has proved a chastening experience. I've never missed anyone or anything so much in my life...'

Jemima suddenly realised that they were having a very private conversation in the corridor and she walked on a few steps and thrust open his bedroom door. 'Never missed anyone...'

Luciano leant back against the door to close it fast behind him. 'Jemima, does it take a hammer to knock an idea into your head?' He groaned. 'I phone you every hour on the hour and you think that's normal? I invite your whole family here to keep you company so that you can't even look at another man while I'm away. Don't you ever get suspicious, *piccolo mia*? You think I don't realise that wet blanket, Steven, is sitting out there waiting for you, hoping like hell that I'll screw up and lose you?'

'But I don't fancy Steven...and even when you upset me or I get annoyed with you, I still fancy you,' Jemima confided a little desperately, because he was smiling that wicked smile of his that made her heart beat crazily fast.

'Is that a fact?' Luciano teased, shifting off the door to shed his jacket and jerk loose his tie. 'I had this unrealistic fantasy where I came home and everything would be all right and we would go straight to bed... Don't know what I thought we'd do with all our guests.'

'Everything *is* all right. Our guests are also remarkably good at entertaining themselves,' she opined. 'Oh, by the way, I love you…loads and loads…and it's got nothing to do with your money like Steven thinks.'

'Honestly…you love me?' Luciano growled. 'But why?'

'That's the weird bit… I truly don't know. One minute I was fancying you like mad and the next I was wanting to make your life perfect for you,' Jemima confided with an embarrassed wince.

'Equally weird for me from the very first moment. Took me a long time to realise that not wanting to love again was basically a fear of being hurt again, which is cowardly,' he declared with disdain. 'And then you were there and I liked just about everything about you and it wasn't only sex. I should've told you the truth about Gigi sooner but I suppose I didn't want you to think less of me.'

'How could I think less of you for her bad behaviour?'

Luciano shrugged. 'I love the way you are with Nicky because she was so cold with Melita. Comparisons are tasteless but…'

'So, don't make them.' Jemima unzipped her dress and shimmied out of it while he watched.

'Your parents…' Luciano began, slightly shocked.

'I think everyone will mind their own business rather than ours,' Jemima whispered sagely. 'But you do realise that you still haven't told me who told you that I was upset?'

Luciano expelled his breath on a slow hiss. 'Your father.'

Taken aback, Jemima blinked. 'Say that again?'

'He thinks I make you happy and he likes the fact that I'm honest with him,' Luciano told her guiltily, as if he had been consorting with the enemy. 'I was grateful that he called me.'

Jemima was secretly pleased that the father she loved so much clearly liked and trusted the man she was about to marry. 'I've got no complaints either. We love each other and that's special.'

'Simply finding you was special, *piccolo mia*,' Luciano told her as she unbuttoned his shirt, undid his waistband, sent her fingers roaming over the prominent bulge at his groin with a daring new to both of them and even more thrilling. '*Dio mio*, I love you…'

'Me too…*so much*,' she managed to say just before his mouth came crashing down on hers with all the passion she adored.

Jemima walked down the aisle of the little village church in her lace wedding dress and with her hand on her father's arm. Off the shoulder and styled with tight sleeves and a fitted bodice, her wedding gown made the most of her hourglass figure and the exquisite lace fell to the floor, showing only the toes of the extravagant shoes she wore.

Luciano was so entranced by the sight of her that he couldn't look away and play it cool. His son, Nicky, sat on his grandmother's lap near the front of the church and began to bounce and hold out his arms when he laid eyes on Jemima, the closest thing to a mother he would ever know. Luciano smiled, the happiest he had ever been in his chequered life and far happier than he had ever even hoped to be.

Jemima focused on the man she loved and her heart jumped behind her breastbone. All hers at last, officially, finally, permanently hers. As if a wedding ring were the equivalent of a padlock, she scolded herself. It was the love she saw in his beautiful dark eyes that would hold him and she rejoiced in the thought of the future that awaited them and their son.

EPILOGUE

'IL CAPO!' AGNESE SIGNALLED Jemima from the door of the castle with a beatific smile that said that all was now right with the housekeeper's world because Luciano was finally home again after a week away on business.

Jemima thought back four years to the days when the elderly Agnese, Luciano's fiercest admirer, had still been unsure of her former charge's second wife. She and Agnese had started out being excruciatingly polite to each other while Jemima had become friendlier with the housekeeper's daughter, Carlotta, whose English had come on as quickly as Jemima's Italian during the first year of her marriage. And then Concetta, their first child, had been born and Agnese had crumbled like a meringue at first sight of Il Capo's daughter to reveal the kindly, loving woman she hid behind her tough little image.

After Concetta, the nursery had got even busier and had had to expand because two children had been born to swell the family. Jemima's second pregnancy had produced twin boys, Marco and Matteo, and she had decided to take a break from the production line for a year or two at least. Three little boys ranging from Nicky, who was almost five, and the twins, who were two years old, had proved quite a handful. Concetta was three, clever and well behaved, certainly easier to control than three rumbustious little boys. Jemima's daughter was very fond of raising her brows in the boys' direction and mimicking her father with an air of female superiority.

Jemima's life had changed so rapidly from the moment she had become a mother for the first time after Nicky that she sometimes could hardly recall the period before she had met Luciano. Real life and fulfilling happiness had begun for her in Sicily at the *castello*. Occasionally she had thought sadly about the job she had left behind, but caring for Nicky had kept her very busy and Concetta's arrival had persuaded Jemima that she was perfectly happy shaping her routine round her husband and children. Such an existence might not be perfect for everyone, but it was perfect for her.

She adored Luciano and she adored her kids and her home and the staff who looked after them so well. She never ever forgot either to be grateful for her good fortune. Luciano had bought a comfortable house for her parents back in the UK, but they remained regular visitors to the island, most often staying in the cottage by the beach. Her husband had become almost as fond of his in-laws as his wife. He appreciated the retired couple's loving interest in their grandchildren and rarely went to the UK without taking them out to dinner. Jemima's friend, Ellie, was a regular visitor as well, but there had been no further contact from Steven, who had married a couple of years back.

Now awaiting Luciano's arrival, Jemima smoothed her hands down over the elegant blue dress she wore with the most ridiculously high heels in her wardrobe. He bought her shoes everywhere he went without her because he knew that, even though she preferred to spend most of her time at home rather than shopping or partying as she could have done, she got a kick out of wearing that kind of footwear. It was the type of thoughtfulness and all the little caring touches that accompanied it that made Jemima such an adoring wife.

The shouts of three little boys backed by the far more muted tones of her little daughter warned Jemima that Luciano was in the hall. She grinned as he raised his voice to be heard above the hubbub and then there was silence, the sound of quick steps across the tiles as he made his escape and the door opened.

And there he stood, her beautiful Luciano, who still thrilled her as much at first glance as he had five years earlier. 'You look very beautiful, Signora Vitale,' he told her teasingly.

She encountered his stunning dark golden eyes and her heart sang as she surged across the room to throw herself into his arms. 'I missed you.'

Luciano gazed down at her with smouldering appreciation. 'The kids are waiting in the hall.'

'They want to see you too.'

'Can't be in two places at once, *amata mia*,' he husked, claiming a passionate kiss with raw, hungry enthusiasm.

'Carlotta will distract them,' Jemima mumbled.

'We're being selfish,' he groaned, lean brown hands worshipping her generous curves. 'But I can't... Bedtime's hours away,' he muttered defensively.

'So it is... I love you,' Jemima confided, enchanted by the level of passionate appreciation in his smouldering scrutiny, for it was wonderful to feel that desirable to the man she loved.

'Not one half as much as I love and need you,' Luciano countered. 'It isn't possible, *amata mia*.'

'What have I told you about that negative outlook of yours?' Jemima censured, backing down on the sofa in what was a decidedly inviting way with happiness and amusement and passion all bubbling up together inside her and making her feel distinctly intoxicated on love.

* * * * *

Don't miss Lynne Graham's stunning 100th book,
BOUGHT FOR THE GREEK'S REVENGE
Coming in June 2016!

MILLS & BOON®
Hardback – April 2016

ROMANCE

The Sicilian's Stolen Son	Lynne Graham
Seduced into Her Boss's Service	Cathy Williams
The Billionaire's Defiant Acquisition	Sharon Kendrick
One Night to Wedding Vows	Kim Lawrence
Engaged to Her Ravensdale Enemy	Melanie Milburne
A Diamond Deal with the Greek	Maya Blake
Inherited by Ferranti	Kate Hewitt
The Secret to Marrying Marchesi	Amanda Cinelli
The Billionaire's Baby Swap	Rebecca Winters
The Wedding Planner's Big Day	Cara Colter
Holiday with the Best Man	Kate Hardy
Tempted by Her Tycoon Boss	Jennie Adams
Seduced by the Heart Surgeon	Carol Marinelli
Falling for the Single Dad	Emily Forbes
The Fling That Changed Everything	Alison Roberts
A Child to Open Their Hearts	Marion Lennox
The Greek Doctor's Secret Son	Jennifer Taylor
Caught in a Storm of Passion	Lucy Ryder
Take Me, Cowboy	Maisey Yates
His Baby Agenda	Katherine Garbera

MILLS & BOON®
Large Print – April 2016

ROMANCE

The Price of His Redemption	Carol Marinelli
Back in the Brazilian's Bed	Susan Stephens
The Innocent's Sinful Craving	Sara Craven
Brunetti's Secret Son	Maya Blake
Talos Claims His Virgin	Michelle Smart
Destined for the Desert King	Kate Walker
Ravensdale's Defiant Captive	Melanie Milburne
The Best Man & The Wedding Planner	Teresa Carpenter
Proposal at the Winter Ball	Jessica Gilmore
Bodyguard...to Bridegroom?	Nikki Logan
Christmas Kisses with Her Boss	Nina Milne

HISTORICAL

His Christmas Countess	Louise Allen
The Captain's Christmas Bride	Annie Burrows
Lord Lansbury's Christmas Wedding	Helen Dickson
Warrior of Fire	Michelle Willingham
Lady Rowena's Ruin	Carol Townend

MEDICAL

The Baby of Their Dreams	Carol Marinelli
Falling for Her Reluctant Sheikh	Amalie Berlin
Hot-Shot Doc, Secret Dad	Lynne Marshall
Father for Her Newborn Baby	Lynne Marshall
His Little Christmas Miracle	Emily Forbes
Safe in the Surgeon's Arms	Molly Evans

0316 GEN STD LP

MILLS & BOON®
Hardback – May 2016

ROMANCE

Morelli's Mistress	Anne Mather
A Tycoon to Be Reckoned With	Julia James
Billionaire Without a Past	Carol Marinelli
The Shock Cassano Baby	Andie Brock
The Most Scandalous Ravensdale	Melanie Milburne
The Sheikh's Last Mistress	Rachael Thomas
Claiming the Royal Innocent	Jennifer Hayward
Kept at the Argentine's Command	Lucy Ellis
The Billionaire Who Saw Her Beauty	Rebecca Winters
In the Boss's Castle	Jessica Gilmore
One Week with the French Tycoon	Christy McKellen
Rafael's Contract Bride	Nina Milne
Tempted by Hollywood's Top Doc	Louisa George
Perfect Rivals...	Amy Ruttan
English Rose in the Outback	Lucy Clark
A Family for Chloe	Lucy Clark
The Doctor's Baby Secret	Scarlet Wilson
Married for the Boss's Baby	Susan Carlisle
Twins for the Texan	Charlene Sands
Secret Baby Scandal	Joanne Rock

MILLS & BOON®
Large Print – May 2016

ROMANCE

The Queen's New Year Secret	Maisey Yates
Wearing the De Angelis Ring	Cathy Williams
The Cost of the Forbidden	Carol Marinelli
Mistress of His Revenge	Chantelle Shaw
Theseus Discovers His Heir	Michelle Smart
The Marriage He Must Keep	Dani Collins
Awakening the Ravensdale Heiress	Melanie Milburne
His Princess of Convenience	Rebecca Winters
Holiday with the Millionaire	Scarlet Wilson
The Husband She'd Never Met	Barbara Hannay
Unlocking Her Boss's Heart	Christy McKellen

HISTORICAL

In Debt to the Earl	Elizabeth Rolls
Rake Most Likely to Seduce	Bronwyn Scott
The Captain and His Innocent	Lucy Ashford
Scoundrel of Dunborough	Margaret Moore
One Night with the Viking	Harper St. George

MEDICAL

A Touch of Christmas Magic	Scarlet Wilson
Her Christmas Baby Bump	Robin Gianna
Winter Wedding in Vegas	Janice Lynn
One Night Before Christmas	Susan Carlisle
A December to Remember	Sue MacKay
A Father This Christmas?	Louisa Heaton

MILLS & BOON®

Why shop at millsandboon.co.uk?

Each year, thousands of romance readers find their perfect read at millsandboon.co.uk. That's because we're passionate about bringing you the very best romantic fiction. Here are some of the advantages of shopping at www.millsandboon.co.uk:

* **Get new books first**—you'll be able to buy your favourite books one month before they hit the shops

* **Get exclusive discounts**—you'll also be able to buy our specially created monthly collections, with up to 50% off the RRP

* **Find your favourite authors**—latest news, interviews and new releases for all your favourite authors and series on our website, plus ideas for what to try next

* **Join in**—once you've bought your favourite books, don't forget to register with us to rate, review and join in the discussions

Visit **www.millsandboon.co.uk**
for all this and more today!

G317